PRIEST-QUEEN

Priest-Queen

A romance: the second in the Goblins and Cheese sequence.

Juniper Butterworth

Other works from this author

Writing as Sharon J. Gochenour

Monsters: A Retelling of Beauty and the Beast

The Threads Quartet
The Golden City
The Golden Empress (coming soon)

Writing as Juniper Butterworth

The Goblins and Cheese sequence
The Changeling

Table of Contents

Content notes

This book contains descriptions of sibling abuse which happened before the story starts, though the abusive sibling in question was being impersonated by a fairy at the time.

I have stewed over how best to write the second part of this note. The short version would probably be "internalized fatphobia, not resolved in the text." Elsyn is a character whose size has been weaponized against her, and she doesn't get over the resulting emotional damage in the space of this book. She gains insight and practice in existing in the world as a fat person, but there is no triumphal moment. Elsyn's internal monologue of shame is a result of the specific abuse and neglect she has experienced, not pervasive cultural hatred of fat people. Other fat people exist in her world without the same level of emotional distress.

PART ONE

Elsyn was pretending she couldn't see the goblin perched in the tree.

Of the twenty-two sacred cows kept by the high temple, six were currently in milk. Pumpkin had twin bull calves and was perfectly happy. Cabbage and Parsnip each had an exceedingly large heifer calf. But Squash and Onion, both prodigious milkers, had produced puny offspring this spring, who could barely empty half their udders. Turnip's calf had been stillborn—harbinger of the awful things the year was to bring, Elsyn thought grimly. So twice daily, Elsyn took out the milking stool and a bucket and herded the milkers into the southern paddock. She took an extra bag of oats to reward the three who didn't need her for letting her check their teats for redness and their milk for lumps.

Five years ago, the temple had kept at least a hundred cattle, but that didn't bear thinking about.

The goblin had folded himself into the branches of a gnarled pine that grew on top of one of the many hillocks that rumpled the holy pasture. He was dark brown and wore dark clothing, so perhaps he thought he would pass for a shadow, pressed against the trunk of the tree.

The tufted tail is rather noticeable, Elsyn thought. Besides that, he was a large creature and didn't fold to a particularly compact size. Perhaps he wasn't used to going among humans.

She wasn't quite used to having goblins in the palace. There had been a small contingent left behind after the coronation three weeks ago, but a second, more numerous group had just arrived the previous night. This fellow was one of the second party.

Elsyn finished with Squash and turned to Onion, shoving a calf's nose away from the bucket.

The goblin had crept out along a branch and peered down toward her when she next caught a glimpse of him out of the corner of her eye.

She took the stool and moved it to Turnip, who shifted and sighed with relief when she started to milk.

"Poor old girl," she muttered, thumping the cow's side affectionately. Turnip had been trying to steal one of Pumpkin's calves since spring, and Pumpkin was having none of it.

When the cow's udder was empty, Elsyn flipped the hinged lid down on the bucket, tucked the stool under her arm, and before she could lose her nerve, strode toward the pine tree.

"Good day to you," she called upward. "Can I help you with something?"

The goblin didn't move.

"I hope you aren't hiding," Elsyn said. "Because I can see you perfectly well."

After a minute the goblin slid down to a lower branch and bent his face toward hers.

It was a striking face, dominated by a pair of enormous orange eyes shot through with amber and gold. He looked very much like a human, though not quite. His nose had a nice arch and sharp divots to either side, and the two tusks protruding from his lower jaw gave his mouth a surly twist. This close, she could see the layer of fine fur covering his skin. His ears were large and pointed, almost cat-like, and the hair on his face rose into a stiff black crest that arched over his skull. The overall effect was handsome but startling.

He balanced on the branch like an acrobat or a leopard, claws on his feet and his hands digging into the bark, his tail held out stiff behind him for balance.

"Sir?" she prompted, when he said nothing.

"When did you learn to milk cows?" the goblin asked, his voice a gravelly baritone.

"I suppose I was thirteen," Elsyn said, flinching a bit at the memory. If this year had been bad, that one had been infinitely worse.

"They listen to you," he said, jerking his chin at Turnip, who had followed Elsyn, lowing mournfully.

"All the priests of the Two-Bodied God can speak to cattle."

"Yes, but they *listen* to you," he repeated. "That big calf could have had the milk out of your bucket ten times, if she'd wanted to."

Elsyn felt her cheeks warm. "Yes, she could have."

"Can you speak with other animals as well, or just cows?"

"Only cows, so far as I know. The older priests told me that they could usually hear goats and deer, but I haven't had a chance to try. That is

—I hear the rats whispering in the granary, and crows laughing, but so does everyone." She felt at a conversational disadvantage with her hands full, so she set down the stool and put the bucket of milk on top of it and then put her hands on her hips. "Are you looking for someone in particular, or just hoping to speak with a priest generally? I don't mean to be rude, but there's barely anyone left in the high temple anymore, and it's not much to look at, if you're wanting to sight-see. We haven't had a high priest since the winter before last." She hesitated, before adding, "The last decade has not been kind to us."

"No one in particular," the goblin said. "Just wandering around."

Kandar had been looking for Elsyn Ardloch, newly-crowned queen of this human country that ran from the mountains in the north and west to the high steppes in the east and down to the sea in the south.

Most significantly to him, it was the country that the goblin road ran into, when it descended from the slightly out-of-register goblin mountains that were just up and to the left of the other range in the north.

He had only a very vague idea of what human queens occupied themselves with, but he did not think it generally included milking cows. He had been told, of course, that Elsyn was a Priest-Queen—the very first in all this realm's history—but somehow his imagination had not stretched to the daily responsibilities of the holy order. Milking seemed like the sort of thing that a person might delegate, once she'd been crowned.

Kandar had been sent south by his cousin the goblin king, whom he loved steadfastly, in service of his queen Taryn, whom Kandar despised. Taryn had spent eleven years under a fairy hill and had correspondingly off-putting habits. She had become something less, or something more, than human during those years, delicately picking her way through fairy magic and fairy politics, being transformed or enchanted on the daily whims of Oberon, the fairy king. Kandar found her itchy on his better days and domineering on her worst. If he were inclined to be honest with himself, which he was not, anything to do with fairies made him nervous.

He had—naturally, he thought—assumed that Taryn's younger sister would be rather like her. It was this assumption that had led him to climb a tree in the paddock where another priest had assured him the young queen was usually to be found in the afternoons. He thought he would learn a great deal about her very quickly when she noticed him.

He might have, but his thoughts became jumbled when Elsyn came over the next hillock, leading a small group of cows. She looked a bit like Taryn, in the sense that a destrier resembles a palfrey; they both had a great mass of black hair, olive complexions, dark brows over great dark eyes, and aquiline noses. Elsyn, however, was a head taller than her sister, with wide shoulders and wide hips under a priest's shift. Taryn had occasional bouts of delicacy, perhaps brought on by many years of restriction and vicious treatment under the fairy hill, but Elsyn looked to be her opposite: a great, powerful, fat woman, the sort of human who could carry a calf under each arm. Her face and shoulders were burnt brown with sun.

She noticed him immediately but got on with milking. The cattle treated her as another cow, one who had oddly chosen to go upright on two legs. They licked her face and chatted with her in small grunts and moos. Each of the sacred cows was a massive beast, with a pair of curving horns that stretched as far above their heads as their backs were above the ground. They observed him, too, with wary intelligence in their large eyes. If he made any impolite advances toward the queen, he would be skewered.

He did not think about anything more for a long while as he watched her intently, until she was standing under the tree, frowning up at him.

"Well," she said finally. "If you're not looking for anyone, perhaps you should come up to the cheesemaking room with me."

"I don't need anyone looking after me," Kandar said. His tail lashed once, involuntarily. That had sounded ruder than he had intended to be.

One corner of Elsyn's mouth tipped up. "No, I'm sure you don't, but if you surprise the bull or the boss cow when you're wandering around, they'll look after you a little less kindly than I will. Besides, there's probably some fresh cheeses that are ready to test."

She picked up the stool and the bucket of milk again and walked uphill, clearly assuming he would follow.

Elsyn was stirring the curds from last night's and this morning's milkings over a small flame when the goblin poked his nose around the workshop door. A second nose followed him, that of a black horse with a white blaze up his face.

Hullo hullo, the horse said. I see you've got very nice cheeses in here, very nice cheeses indeed, I don't suppose any are for horses though, none for horses at all...

"You are correct, none are for horses," Elsyn said firmly, hooking the long cheese spoon from the side of the pot and blocking the door. Delight fluttered in her stomach. She *could* talk to other animals! And this one spoke so clearly. Usually the cows were quite vague.

The goblin squatted down by the door to the aging room—mostly empty, these days—and watched her with a bemused expression.

"Do you want some oats, though?" she went on.

Oh yes, I like oats, oats are very nice. The horse lipped her hands and then her cheek. Where are the oats?

"Stir the curds, please," Elsyn said and handed the goblin the cheese spoon, a little stunned by her own calm. Cheese wasn't to be trusted to any scabby old goblin who wandered into the temple. But it seemed rude to simply ignore the horse—who was, after all, just as much a guest of the palace.

The horse was only too happy to follow her down the length of the temple to one of the grain stores. When the changeling queen had closed the priest-door so the temple could no longer receive shipments of grain from outside the palace, the priests had cordoned off one of the paddocks to grow their own. On the wet, cold hilltop, oats were the only thing that would take, and so they harvested a few bushels each year, stored in the back of the temple and protected by a family of square-faced black cats.

It will be different soon, Elsyn reminded herself. It is my job to *make* it different.

She closed the half-door on the store, leaving Socks in the main hall, and greeted two of the cats sprawled over the tops of the grain bins. She wasn't sure if she couldn't hear their voices because cats and cows were terribly different, or because they didn't choose to speak with her. One of the cats stood, arched her back, and chirped at Socks, who stretched his neck over the half-door to touch his large nose to her small one.

"What's your friend's name?" she asked, offering him a bucket.

Oh yes oats, these are very good oats, I love oats, Socks said. His name is not oats. His name is Kandar son of Usdar daughter of Erlar daughter of Xhindar daughter of Osar daughter of Haldar...

Elsyn's neck prickled uncomfortably. Haldar was the namesake ancestor of the goblin king. She had been told this by the wizard he had sent to the coronation, Ildar.

When she and the horse returned to the workshop the goblin had hunched himself over the cheese pot, poking individual curds with the tip of the spoon.

She's very nice, she has oats in a bucket, *you* should ask her for oats in a bucket, Socks informed the goblin.

Elsyn firmly shut the workshop door in the horse's face—"I'm sorry, we'll be done in just a minute"—took the spoon from Kandar, and scooped out a curd to squeeze it between her two fingers. She popped it in her mouth thoughtfully. "This is pretty close to done. I should get the salt out. Do you want a piece?"

When he nodded stiffly, she spooned out a bit more cheese, flipped it onto her fingers to drain, and offered it to him. He looked confused for a minute, before leaning forward and delicately taking it from her hand in his teeth.

Elsyn turned away to hide her red face. "Do you like it?" she asked the cheese pot, watching him from the corner of her eye.

He swallowed slowly and licked his lips. "I'm not sure. I've only had horse milk."

She hummed as she unfolded a cheese cloth from the cabinet and laid it inside a metal basket that hung in the mouth of a large crock. She wrapped her shift around her hands to take the pot off the fire, remembering a moment too late how that motion hiked the fabric up high over her legs. She flinched and quickly poured the curds into the strainer.

I'll throw this pot at his head if he says anything, she thought. *I will.* I'm the queen now and no one is going to say anything about tree trunks to me ever again.

Kandar's brain fizzed to a halt as his eyes traced the rise of the hem of Elsyn's shift up the back of her thighs.

Some minutes later, a single, pathetic thought struggled its way to the churning surface.

This is not how I expected her to be.

"What does horse cheese taste like?" Elsyn asked.

Kandar grunted. "Uh. It doesn't really make … cheese, in the same way. It sort of, uh, bubbles up. Like beer."

She heard the sound of claws on the stone floor, and suddenly he was peering over her shoulder into the strainer.

"What happens now?" His breath tickled her ear.

"I mix in salt with the curds and put them in the press."

"How long are they. Uh. In the press?"

"A day or so, until most of the whey is pressed out."

Can I drink the whey? Socks asked from the other side of the closed door. I would like to drink the whey, it smells very nice, I have heard that whey is very good for horses.

Elsyn laughed. "No, we use it for our breakf—" She turned her face toward the door without thinking, and her nose bumped into the goblin's nose. He was taller than she was, but he had bent down low to get a better look at the draining curds over her shoulder.

He didn't move. She thought she should probably move, but instead she stayed where she was, the tip of her nose touching the side of his nose. Her stomach was doing a very strange thing.

Hello, hello, I am still on the other side of this door, which is still very closed, I am very bored and lonely, please come right away because I think I might need to go chew on something, Socks said.

I should go stop him from getting into mischief, Elsyn thought vaguely.

Kandar probably had the same thought; his head turned toward the door as well, leaving Elsyn with her nose in the space under his ear.

He smells nice, Elsyn thought wistfully. Like sweet grass. Almost like a cow. I suppose that's what horses smell like.

The goblin's clawed hand came to rest on her waist. For a moment, she thought about how lovely, how easy it would be to relax against that hand and that shoulder. She had felt like a wire stretched to breaking for—well, if she were honest, years now. It would be nice to relax somewhere, with someone.

It was a very brief moment. The hand reminded her of her body, of what had been said to her about her body, of why no one was going to ever say anything to her about it again.

She was a queen. And as a queen, she probably shouldn't be

messing about with a goblin in the temple's cheesemaking workshop. It wasn't as if she knew him or could trust him.

Elsyn took a half-step back. "Pardon me."

"Pardon," the goblin repeated. He seemed to come back to himself and ducked his head in a little bow. "I will go look after Socks." He rose to his full height and looked down on her through inscrutable orange eyes. "It was … interesting … to meet you."

The goblin delegation had taken over one of the lower sections of the palace, a chain of rooms immediately adjoining the stables and far distant from the royal residence and the temple on the top of the hill. To return from the temple, Kandar and Socks had to pass first through the pastures, then the ancient, cavernous throne room, bypassing the monarch's rooms to descend multiple terraces of noble apartments, public rooms, kitchens, great halls, and courtyards, before arriving in the lowest section, dedicated to service rooms, laundries, storage, and workshops, built against the exterior wall. The palace was a small dysfunctional town in of itself.

Kandar had noted uneasily how many different social machines ran within its walls—the large body of servants in dark blue livery, associated with the palace itself; a smaller group of serving people wearing black, employed to look after the aristocratic families staying there; and the nobles themselves, most of whom still stank of fairy glamour. He couldn't tell how many families were represented within these walls, but he and Socks surprised three different groups of finely-dressed humans ascending the palatial staircases while they descended.

All of it contrasted painfully with the empty, dusty, decidedly unmagical smell of the temple on the hill above. He had seen four other priests after Elsyn, and they had hurried away as soon as they noticed him.

Socks led him into the stables, where the goblins had taken the doors off several stalls and hoisted the grain bins into the rafters to protect them from magical horses. Socks could open locked doors and untie knots, and he was not the most intelligent of the goblin mounts.

Kandar found what he was looking for perched atop a pile of boards, fastidiously washing its ears with one paw. The cat paused, considering him with green eyes, before busily attacking its left flank with bristling tongue. He would have asked one of the temple cats, but god-infused places made magic go strange and faint.

"I have a message for the goblin king," he told the cat, offering a claw to sniff. The cat, a dark tortoiseshell, deigned to nose his knuckle, before rubbing its—no, her—face vigorously against his hand.

"You honor me," Kandar said gravely.

The cat sat perfectly upright, curling her tail over her white forepaws.

"Tell the king that Taryn's sister hasn't got the fairy-stench on her," he said. More words fought to get out of his mouth, some sensible —everything else reeks of fairies here; I don't trust any of the humans in the palace; why is the temple so empty?—and some decidedly not—Why didn't you warn me that Elsyn is magnificent?

Whatever he said, he reminded himself, would be heard not only by his cousin but also Taryn, and most likely by Ashmallen, the forest witch, beloved of both. He did not care if he offended Taryn, but the goblin king and Ash cared very much.

Finally he said, "Elsyn makes very good cheese," and made a half-bow to the cat.

She tucked her chin against her chest for moment, then jumped down from the boards and vanished around the corner.

"Maybe we shouldn't just give advice on who we think the queen should marry," Kandar said. "Maybe we should put forward someone." He stood in the innermost room of the goblin quarters, the only one with no windows and a door that could be shut tight, with five other members of the delegation.

Ildar, the goblin king's wizard, stared at him, his mouth slightly open. He had led the first delegation of goblins to attend the coronation and had stayed on to supervise ongoing diplomatic relations—which, as the king had very pointedly *not* said before they left, meant ensuring the fairies had really left the palace.

Ildar was the last of the horse-lords who had ridden over the mountains into the goblin kingdom many hundreds of years ago, though he had made the journey in a baby bundle on his mother's back. Kandar had been in deepest awe of him from childhood, until circumstances had conspired to demand that he rescue Ildar from the clutches of a powerful nettle spirit. The wizard had tried to harvest her abode for soup. Now

Kandar only felt a manageable amount of awe.

"And who do you think that should be?" Jolar asked. Jolar was another cousin to the king on his father's side. She had four husbands and had once killed a dragon by hurling a wagon wheel through the air and decapitating it. Kandar had been in love with her several times, though he hadn't mentioned it after the first time, when she had fallen off her horse laughing.

Ildar's mouth snapped shut. "Yes, who?"

"It should be me," Kandar said. "I'm the closest to the king by blood and by foster." His mother Usdar was the only blood-sister of the old queen. "It would be an insult to offer anyone of lower rank."

Usdar had generally been an absent parent, fighting trolls and bog wights and occasionally minor gods, so Kandar had spent all of his childhood and most of his youth following the king like a hound. She was an illustrious parent to have, if only she had been home long enough to teach him anything.

Ildar, Jolar, and the other three goblins looked blankly at him. If they were thinking of his complaints over the past three weeks about being named emissary to the human kingdom—which had continued during the ride down, right up to the morning before he had gone out to sit in the tree to watch Elsyn—none of them said anything.

Jolar was possibly considering the arrogance of a husband offering himself up instead of waiting to be chosen.

"What?" Ildar said.

"The presentation of the first princeling and the dukes who are asking after her hand is tomorrow afternoon," Kandar went on. "I'll put myself forward then. It's a good match. The queen needs allies, and we are a very good ally."

"*What?*" Ildar said.

"I'm the best choice," Kandar said. "I'll be the only one there who hasn't done any treason."

The tortoiseshell cat was waiting for Kandar just outside the goblin quarters, batting a piece of lint lazily across the floor.

He crouched and blinked slowly at her.

She blinked slowly at him, opening her mouth as if to meow.

The goblin king's voice, lower and less gravelly than Kandar's own, emanated from somewhere behind the feline teeth. "Keep watch for fairy doors. Oberon may have opened others into the city. Try not to annoy Jolar too much." The cat closed her mouth and dabbed a paw to the lint.

Kandar was preparing to feel embarrassed and annoyed—trust his cousin to use part of the message to tease him—when the cat meowed again.

"Ash wants to know if Elsyn ages her cheeses, or makes only fresh. Taryn begs that you take care of her sister, as she was not able to."

Kandar looked sharply at the cat, who twitched her ears and sauntered away.

The royal headdress was extremely heavy, and it took Elsyn a few tries to get it settled so it didn't chafe. It was gold on gold, a heavy band studded with red stones wrapped around the base of the priest horns. The horns were hollow but still massive. The whole contraption was so tall that she had to take it off again to walk through the door.

She had not really believed she was going to be crowned. She still didn't really believe that it had happened now. She was the spare daughter, the lesser daughter, the daughter who had been given to the temple ten years ago to spare her parents further embarrassment. When the heir had been Taryn, who was perfect, beautiful, everything they could have wanted, how could anyone imagine another queen? Once Taryn herself had bored of having her younger sister around, there was no reason for their parents not to hustle Elsyn off to the holy cowherds.

But now, Taryn was gone. As far as the rest of the kingdom knew, she had been kidnapped by fairies and then killed trying to escape. Fairies were vicious. Everyone knew that.

Elsyn examined her reflection grimly. She had known, she thought, though she kept that thought hidden at the back of her mind, as if someone might overhear. She had known something was wrong when Taryn stopped protecting her. The first time her sister had laughed when one of her mother's ladies had called her fat, she had *known*.

She had just turned thirteen, and Taryn fifteen. Before then, the comments about her body had been part of a larger game, where the noble women competed to say the nastiest thing possible about each other's children, phrased as a compliment. The game started when the queen left the salon for her afternoon audiences and ended when Taryn got angry, usually a few minutes after they started needling Elsyn.

She couldn't remember the exact wording of the insult. She did remember the precise distance her stomach had dropped when, at the moment that Taryn always snarled, "*Stop* that," she instead laughed a weird, tinkling laugh.

The feeling of betrayal had not left her. Maybe it would never leave.

It had only gotten worse, as Taryn—the false Taryn, the fairy Taryn, the impostor Taryn—had gotten more and more slender, and Elsyn had grown fatter and fatter. The ladies scrabbling to get into the heir's good graces found they could garner favor by making much of the difference. This version of Taryn hadn't even cared if they repeated their witticisms about pigs and bridge piers.

In some way Elsyn had been relieved when her parents had given her up as a priest. Certainly it meant hard labor—cleaning the barn, carrying hay, often milking cows who would prefer not to be milked—and less comfort—she'd slept in the cold dormitory with the other priests and worn the same linen shift they all wore. But no one mocked her or yelled at her or invented cruel games that she couldn't refuse to play and always lost.

She had tried to grieve when her parents had died suddenly two years later, the year Taryn had turned eighteen, but when she looked into her heart all she found was coldness. She had attended the state funeral as part of the block of priests, with no more concession to her relation to the dead than a black armband, and when she looked at the caskets she felt nothing.

The deprivations of temple life had grown sharply worse after Taryn had been crowned. She had shut the priest-gate and barred the temple from receiving grain or hay or medicines that had not passed through the palace first and received her approval. Most things had not been given that stamp and were sent back, and after a year of this merchants did not even try to sell to the temple anymore. The temple had once been a center of worship, of medicine, of legal and veterinary assistance, but no more. The hardest blow had struck the year before, when a cattle plague had killed thousands of animals up and down the country and diminished the holy herd itself by sixty beasts.

And now both Taryns are gone, and I am queen, Elsyn thought. What had really happened before her coronation was too bewildering to contemplate.

She smoothed the fabric of her new robe down her thighs, admiring the golden patterns woven in among the white threads. It was cut to resemble the priest's shift, but the fabric was thick and lined so that it fell away from her body in a smooth waterfall. So far, the appointment with the tailor was the only one she had made herself as queen.

"Your Majesty," came a voice from the door. "The reception room is ready."

I'm not ready! Elsyn gave her head a little shake to clear out that thought. The horns of the headdress sliced through the air. The lady at the door blanched and backed away. She was short and as fine-boned as a child, and Elsyn felt like a hulking monster standing before her.

I think I recognize this one, Elsyn thought, falling in behind her. She used to sit right next to Taryn and bray like a donkey whenever a joke was made about me. No wonder she's frightened now.

Little does she know that I've no friends. Taryn—the fairy—made sure of that. I doubt anyone will so much as lift a finger if I start giving out orders. The High Priest might have helped me, but they're gone, too.

The lady stopped by a door and bowed to her. Elsyn took off the headdress, walked through the door, and put it back on.

There were four lords and five ladies already in the room, as well as two blank-faced servants in black livery. Elsyn's heart sank as she looked over them. Two of the lords and the four of the ladies had been toadies for Taryn. The others she didn't recognize, though they all looked very small. With the horns, she towered over everyone in the room.

She did not sigh.

They were all bowing now and murmuring polite things. A lady with a pearled stomacher pinned to the front of her gown gestured gracefully to her. Elsyn thought she had been the one to organize this reception, and she dug around in her head for a name. Ilana? Ilana of … something. Glascrann, maybe.

The assembled were murmuring.

"It would be good to get this settled."

"Of course one worries about an heir."

"If only *she* had married. . . "

Elsyn fixed this last lady with a bleak stare, and she withered.

"Go on then," she said, more gruffly than she would have liked. "Bring in the suitors."

The four hopefuls walked in, each dressed a little more grandly than the last. One was old, fifty or even sixty. One had a religious medallion pinned ostentatiously on the front of his cloak, but it wasn't for the Two-Bodied God. One had a goatee. One was young and red-faced. They were all shorter than her. The young one was *much* shorter than her.

It wasn't that she minded, Elysn thought mutinously. Only that short men minded *her*.

The various nobles started to make the case for and against each of the men. Elsyn half-listened and imagined what Pumpkin or Turnip would think of each of them.

A little snort of laughter bubbled up—she tried to swallow it—

The door flew open again. In marched Ildar, the wizard, his face ablaze with purpose. He had been responsible for fusing the crown to the priest's horns. He was a lanky individual, so tall that she felt squat in comparison, and oddly gray in his coloration: gray skin, gray hair, gray eyes, gray vest and tunic over gray pantaloons. Behind him were six goblins all dressed in brilliant colors and carrying long, curved swords.

"We wish to offer a suitor," the wizard said, in a ringing voice.

"Oh, but—"

"Goblins don't—"

"Surely not—"

"You can't be serious," the man with the goatee said. "A goblin can't marry a human. There would be no issue."

"My mother was human," came a gravelly baritone from near the door.

"I present our suitor, Prince Kandar, son of Usdar, daughter of Erlar—" Ildar intoned.

The other five goblins parted, neatly, as though they had practiced this entrance, and the goblin who had watched her from the apple tree stalked forward. His vest, tunic, and trousers were all flame red. The wizard went on intoning, listing the names and lineages of all the other goblins present.

Elsyn bit back one response, then another, then another—you're a *prince?*—oh, so you weren't looking for anyone in particular, *hm?*—why are you *here?*—before taking a deep breath. If she hadn't been so angry, his splendor would have been intimidating. She knew from standing close to him that he did not have a delicate frame, but his great height and the brilliant sash wrapped tightly around his midsection made him seem like a slash of motion through the air.

"I recognize the prince's right to present his suit," she said evenly.

She met his orange eyes.

He smelled nice, Elsyn remembered wistfully. Like a cow. It would be good to be married to someone who smelled nice.

She shook herself—it was no good making decisions based on how people smelled—but how could she decide? There was no one she trusted in the palace, at least no one who walked on two legs, and there hadn't been for a long time. Most of the priests she had been trained by and with had vanished or escaped. Even in the first years of the false Taryn's reign, before the temple had been emptied out, the High Priest wouldn't have had much to say about picking out a husband. And before that—before that—

A bit of what one of the ladies was saying penetrated her dense thoughts. "Raymarell of the line of Deragcaish—not the disgraced branch of the family, of course—"

Deragcaish. *Well.*

"I have decided how I will make my choice," she announced, cutting off the lady in mid-syllable.

"By the respective merits of their bloodlines, yes—" the lady said, trying to get her back on track.

"No," Elsyn said firmly. "I will marry whoever finds Albenyssar of Deragcaish and brings him back to the palace alive and in good health."

The assembled nobles stared at her as though she had asked them to find unicorn dung and smear themselves with it.

"You may go," Elsyn said.

Kandar found a large black tom in a courtyard near the stables, sitting on the edge of a fountain and drinking. The cat accepted a bite of cheese and a scratch behind the ears.

"I have a message for the goblin king," he told the cat.

The tom jumped down to the cobbles and arranged himself in a listening position, pupils huge, ears pricked.

"Tell my cousin that I am going to marry Elsyn," Kandar said. He considered trying to explain why, then decided that the king had married Taryn and ought to understand. "I have to complete a simple task for her first—" Though the mountains-just-to-the-left were hundreds of miles and a plain of reality away, he thought he could hear his cousin, who had rescued him from a half-dozen *simple tasks,* more than one involving trolls, laughing uproariously. "—but it will be done soon enough. Tell Ash I have only seen Elsyn make fresh cheese so far. Jolar and Ildar will stay with the new queen while I am gone." He hesitated, then said finally, "Tell Taryn I will do my best to take care of her."

The cat stretched, rubbed along his ankles, and disappeared through a doorway.

Kandar and Socks rode east. They passed fields of wheat and pastures, which eventually became pastures and meadows, which eventually became open grassland. Shortly after that the road ran out.

Socks, who was the son and grandson and great-grandson of powerful and wise horses, even if he was not one himself, ran over the grass like a ship skimming over the waves. He was very excited about having an adventure and kept up a stream of commentary about every new and interesting smell that came to his nose.

There is a cow! That is also a cow! And there is a calf with that cow, and there is another cow and also a bull, there are some goats *and there is a horse!* Two goats—

Kandar, who was used to Socks' monologue, brooded over what he had learned about Albenyssar of Deragcaish.

No one in the palace had wanted to talk about Albenyssar, including the few priests in the temple he had been able to corner. Jolar, who had taken up drinking in the city every evening, came back with a grim expression and little news.

"No one wants to say," she told the goblins together. "But he would have been lord of a high house, were he not banished several years back for some sort of crime against another lordling."

"Banished by the changeling queen," Ildar clarified.

Jolar nodded. "As soon as she'd gotten rid of the old queen and her consort and been crowned herself."

Now, as the grass rippled around him in red-gold waves, Kandar wondered what the trumped-up charge had been. He wondered what threat Albenyssar had posed to the changeling queen. He wondered why Elsyn wanted him back, and how she had known him. He was not jealous, because it would be foolish to be jealous of a man he did not know over a woman he had just met, but he felt rather sour as he wondered.

It had taken a few more nights of Jolar drinking in various taverns, occasionally bringing along her niece Fenar and her nephew Emar —Kandar had been in love with both of them of too, with somewhat more success—before they had gathered enough information to give

Kandar a direction to follow.

"We fell in with some army captains this evening," Fenar had explained. "Some of them had known Albenyssar; he went straight from his mother's house into a soldier's uniform. They said he wasn't exactly banished—there's apparently some myth of monsters living past the grasslands in the east. He was told to go kill them all and come back with evidence he'd done it. Of course, given that monsters may not have ever existed—"

A bit like the quest I'm on now, Kandar thought. No hope of success. Even if this fellow is out here somewhere, he's got thousands of miles of open country to lose himself. And he might be dead. He sighed and settled deeper into the saddle. If he couldn't find Albenyssar in a few weeks, he would circle back to the capital and figure out a different way to get close to Elsyn. Maybe he could bargain with her for cheeses.

There's a different sort of grass up ahead, Socks informed him. It smells like *licorice*.

"Sounds nice," Kandar muttered. What did humans want in exchange for their cheeses? he thought. What did Elsyn want? What could he possibly give her?

Suddenly his horse was turning and coming to a stop. Here! Here is the nice grass!

Kandar poked him in the shoulder and then in the belly, but Socks had his head down, munching. Sighing, the goblin vaulted off his back and landed in a crouch, before standing to look around.

He paused. The grass they had been riding through for most of the afternoon had been golden, browned by months of hot sun, with only the faintest hints of green deep among the stalks. It was shoulder-high, and without Socks' magical pedigree it would have been slow going indeed to cross through it.

But here, Socks had found a little tongue-shaped patch of green, short grass growing among the brown, which he was now devouring with enthusiasm.

The patch continued on for several feet. It smelled strange and felt strange. Kandar knelt and sniffed it. It wasn't just that the grass was new, perhaps the result of a small fire or lightning strike; it was an entirely different sort of plant from those growing either side of it.

Then he looked up. To his left, the strip of green grass continued into the horizon, sliding into a vertical gray slit in the brilliant, hard blue sky. He rose and walked toward the slit. A gust of cold, salty air blew toward him from that slice of gray sky, in contrast to the hot, muggy air over the grasslands.

Socks put his head up and his ears forward, curious. Is that another goblin road? he asked.

"I think it is," Kandar said. A little break in the world, he thought, that goes to a different, greener grassland just up and to the left. And what an *interesting* place for there to be monsters hiding, or one out-of-favor noble. "We'll go this way."

The morning after Kandar rode east, Ildar and another goblin visited Elsyn in the temple fields. She was in the northeast paddock, the one a little bit behind the temple, talking with Bean, the Boss Cow.

Talking was perhaps not the right word. Bean was older and less vague than the other cows, but she communicated primarily in forceful bovine aphorisms. She liked Elsyn enormously, but she also regarded her as an upstart young heifer who didn't know anything about leading a herd. It helped Elsyn's understanding a bit if she could lay hands on the Boss Cow's hide. Bean tolerated this with good grace.

She saw the wizard and his companion approaching through the grass out of the corner of her eye, but Bean was about to declaim, so she did not turn to face them. The goblin with him was not so tall as Kandar, but her crest and the fur on her face were a striking chestnut color. Elsyn shuffled through names in her memory and came up with *Jolar*.

HORNS OUT, ASSES IN, Bean thundered. WOLVES SOON KNOW WHAT'S ABOUT.

Ildar and Jolar stopped and looked at each other, then looked at Elsyn and Bean.

"She's dispensing her wisdom," Elsyn said. "You have to wait a bit."

GRASS GROWS BEST WHERE FIRE HAS BEEN, Bean went on.

"My mum told me that one," Jolar said.

Bean considered this, stuck her tongue in one nostril, and regurgitated some cud.

"Do you hide up here all the time?" Ildar asked.

Elsyn took her palms off the cow's back, stung. "I'm not *hiding*."

Both of them stared at her. Belatedly, it occurred to Elsyn that being ignored in favor of a cow might offend a certain sort of person.

"The only way I can be sure none of Taryn's—it is best if I avoid the old queen's associates," she said stiffly. "I may be queen, but no one concerns themselves with my wishes." She wished immediately that she could stuff those words back in her mouth, but it wasn't as if it were a secret that she had no noble allies.

"That," said Ildar, "is what we would like to speak to you about."

Elsyn folded her arms, hoping she looked stern rather than anxious. "What do you mean?"

Jolar shrugged. She was nearly as large as Elsyn; it was only next to Ildar that she looked short. "The goblin king has no desire to control your kingdom," the goblin said. "No one except the fairies wants to watch you all tear yourselves apart."

"I take your word," Elsyn said. "And how would you help me—us to avoid that?"

"We are working at something of a disadvantage," Jolar went on. "We know very little of your court, or your family."

"Or your temple," Ildar broke in. "There were dozens of priests present at your coronation, but we've seen almost none in the palace, and you're up here alone. Where are the high priests? Were any of them under the control of Oberon's daughter?"

Elsyn let her hands fall to her sides, her fists clenched. Her heart beat very loudly in her ears. Ildar's were good questions, and she wished she had ready answers. The evening following the coronation, after the servants had taken the horned crown and special robe away to be stored, she had sat alone in her parents' bedchamber, staring at the door, waiting for someone—anyone—to come speak with her. Hours passed, the light migrating across the bedspread until it faded to dusty shadows, and no one had come. She had finally fallen asleep in her clothes.

"Priests are not touched by fairy magic," she said, struggling to keep her voice even. Maybe if they were more susceptible to glamouring, she thought bitterly, more of them would have survived. She turned to Jolar. "I have not been in the court for a long time. I can tell you who I particularly despised as a child, but no more than that."

Ildar started, " When you marry our cousin—"

A flood of anger rushing through Elsyn. *When you you marry our cousin*, echoed in her head, but it became, *when you are sent to the temple, when you are out of the way, when you are crowned*. She could not remember the last time someone had asked her what she planned to do instead of telling her what they expected of her.

"You are sure of your kinsman," she snapped. An image of the red-clad Kandar stalking with feline grace toward her flashed through her mind, followed quickly by one of him delicately taking a piece of curd from her fingers with his teeth. She hurried on. "There are four others who might yet bring back Be—Albenyssar." Might bring him back, *if* any of the other suitors even meant to make an attempt, *if* Ben were still alive somewhere, *if*—Elsyn could not bear to finish that thought. "Do not presume to tell me my future."

"We are extremely sure," Ildar said. Elsyn thought of the dark form of the goblin perched in the tree above her, crouched like a great cat ready to leap. "You will not be allowed to go back on your word when he returns with the man you asked him to find."

Elsyn's face flushed, and she reached for Bean, who tossed her great horned head and stamped her foot.

The goblin and the wizard backed away. Jolar threw Ildar a look before turning back to Elsyn. "There is much we still ought to discuss—"

"I think we have discussed enough," Elsyn said tightly. "Let us await the return of your prince."

Jolar made a noise like a growl. Bean lowed deep and took a meaningful step forward. The goblin fell back again. "Your Majesty, we do not mean to offend. It is—we wish you to succeed."

You wish for *someone* to succeed, Elsyn thought, exhausted. It doesn't matter if it's me. She stared back, stone-faced.

Jolar unlooped a small object from her belt and offered it on a flat palm. "A token," she said, in the tones of one who has lost control of the conversation. "As a gesture of our—faith. If you wish to speak further on these matters, you know where to find us."

If I take it, maybe this conversation can be over, Elsyn thought. She delicately plucked the object from the goblin's hand.

It was a tiny knife, the blade no longer than Elsyn's palm, encased in a leather sheath. Her gaze shot back up and met the wizard Ildar's inscrutable eyes.

"Good day, your dignities," she said, wishing she knew what form of address goblins used.

"Good day, Your Majesty," Jolar said. Both of them turned to go.

PART TWO

The magic road out of the grasslands led into a very different landscape of short, wet, violently green grass. Blue mountains rose in the near distance and the air smelled like salt. A faint path, no wider than a sheep track, led up and over the closest hill.

Socks followed Kandar through and immediately began to gambol, bucking and kicking and throwing himself down to roll.

This was the price of riding Socks, and he had maintained admirable manners up until now. Kandar put his face near the path and inhaled deeply. A goblin's sense of smell was as acute as a dog's, if not keyed to the same odors.

What scent roiled up from the grass was bewildering, and he scratched at the dirt, trying to release more of it. It smelled like … a goblin, but more specifically, a goblin he did not personally know.

Could it be a troll, or some fairy under a geis to appear as a goblin? he wondered, following the trail on hands and feet up the hill. The last goblin I know of who left our kingdom altogether was Holpar, and he was definitely eaten by something with tentacles.

It was hard to say whether Kandar or the goblin he ran into just over the crest of the hill was more surprised. The other goblin had been squatting down, watching a flock of goats graze. They jumped upright, putting a hand to their blade, and Kandar jumped upright, putting a hand to his blade.

"What," Kandar said out loud. "Who are you?"

The other goblin, whose facial fur was still very light and whose tusks were very small, bobbed their head, as though uncertain whether to duck it respectfully or jut their lower jaw out in a threat display. "Who are *you*? You're trespassing on the goblin road!"

"I *am* a goblin, twit. I can't trespass in goblin territory."

"What clan are you, then?" they demanded, their voice wavering. They were really extremely young, he realized.

"Why are you out here alone?" he asked. "You don't know what might come through on an open road. Where's your foster sib?"

A blade jabbed into the base of his skull. Right. The foster sib was behind him.

"You didn't answer the question," a deep voice said. He thought the blade poking him was probably a spear. "What clan are you?"

Oh, they think *I'm* the fairy, come to steal their babies and poison their old, Kandar thought. Serves me right. "My name is Kandar, son of Usdar … " He went through his lineage until Haldar, and then added, "I am foster brother to the king of goblins and sent to retrieve Albenyssar of Deragcaish, by order of the Queen Elsyn Ardloch."

Before he could say any more, the blade came away from his neck, and the haft of the spear knocked him sprawling. The young goblin, who until this moment had wavered uncertainly, drew their long-knife and pointed it at him.

"What do you want with Ben?"

"*Telred*," said the deeper goblin voice, exasperated. Kandar turned his head and saw that this voice came from a huge female goblin wearing a lot of silver jewelry. "You shouldn't have said anything."

Socks chose this moment to rejoin him, leaping down from the hill. What are you doing! This is *my* goblin! I will kick you with my very sharp hooves!

"Another horse!" Telred yelped.

"Socks, *don't*," Kandar bellowed, diving forward before the horse could lunge at the big goblin and get a spear in the side for his trouble. He grabbed the bridle and held his nose down for a minute, until Socks grudgingly agreed not to bite, strike, or body-slam anyone without giving Kandar fair warning first. "I wish your friend no harm," he said, enunciating each syllable very carefully. "Only to speak with him and explain what has come to pass while he has been away. I have given you my true name and lineage, and I request your hospitality."

The younger goblin looked unconvinced, but the big goblin raised her spear point a bit from pointing directly at Kandar's heart. "Fine," she said ungraciously. "You can plead your case with the witan." She gestured along the narrow path with her spear. "This way."

After a restless night punctuated by bad dreams, Elsyn decided she could waste no more time wandering the temple and the royal quarters alone. The meeting with the goblins had gone very badly. She had not meant to refuse their help; she had lost control of her mouth after the wizard had spoken so condescendingly to her. She could not afford to lose her temper like that again.

It was not as if she had a better option that the prince Kandar. Of the nobles who had presented themselves as suitors, he was certainly the least likely to knife her in her sleep. That he was also very nice to look at and smelled good and spoke with animals was, comparatively, unimportant. The thought of being married at all made her feel quite ill. People who were that close invariably vanished just when you needed them most, she thought. Or turned into someone else entirely.

She had run through every living relation she had in a litany, trying to pick out one she thought she could ask for help. The trouble was that none of them knew her, and she knew none of them, after ten years spent isolated in the temple. They might have been favorites of the false Taryn, or friends of her favorites.

If she were married to Kandar, she could ask him to investigate the secrets of her nobles.

If Kandar found Ben and brought him back, she'd have at least one person she trusted close by.

She smashed that thought back down into darkness. Kandar would not find Ben.

That left her with the priests, at least those priests still living. After the fairy impostor had taken the throne, the number of deadly accidents befalling the holy orders had suddenly increased. There had been three years where almost every week a priest had gotten run down by a wagon or kicked in the head by a wild horse. Others had simply … vanished. The old courier routes running from temple to temple had faded away, and no one could tell them what was happening in the countryside.

Then the High Priest had gone, and silence had descended over the few remaining on the palace grounds.

Elsyn decided she should start with Neddie, the high temple's accountant. Neddie was a woman of indeterminate age, older than forty and likely younger than eighty, with pale hair clipped short and a permanently glum expression etched into her face. Everyone knew that as a novice, Neddie had forgotten a ledger of debts owed to various merchants in the southwest pasture, where it had been eaten by Tulip, the old bull. This was the last interesting thing that Neddie had done, and this lack of any apparent personality was probably the reason she had survived the false Taryn's cull.

Boringness, Elsyn thought irritably, and an almost equal slipperiness. In the normal way of things, she often caught glimpses of white hair or the shadow of a skinny arm through doorways and around corners, but the accountant proved to be almost impossible to find when one was actively looking for her. The other priests all looked vague and embarrassed when she questioned them about Neddie's whereabouts.

Neddie had worked closely with the last high priest, and the high priest before them. She had known all the merchants selling goods to the temple and all the wealthy who had made donations in return for care of their cattle, their dogs, and their children. If there was anyone left who knew where priests might have been disappeared to, or where they might have chosen to disappear themselves, it would be the accountant.

But Neddie was not to be found by lying in wait in the temple refectory, combing every temple store room, or by jabbing at the holy hay stacks with a long stick and a dubious expression. Three days passed before Elsyn spotted a shaven pale head in an odd place: stepping into a scullery outside an auxiliary palace kitchen.

Elsyn plunged through the door after her, thinking, Is she tallying up the spoons? Why would Neddie be in the palace at all?

The room was empty. This was not the main scullery, or one of the major minor sculleries; there were a few dusty crocks under the counter and some large soup tureens stacked on the shelves above. One of them was cracked.

Where had Neddie gone?

Elsyn bit her lip in frustration, sucking in air through her nose and holding it. In that pause between breaths, a faint sound caught her ear —voices. There must be servants coming down the hallway behind her, she thought, looking over her shoulder. But there was no one in the passage.

The murmuring continued, but it wasn't coming from down the hall. Elsyn walked back into the scullery, frowning. The voices were coming from behind the shelf with the tureens stacked behind it.

From the next room? No, the walls of the palace were stone, and sound hardly passed through them. There must be an opening somewhere.

She touched the wall behind the shelves, lightly tapping her fingers along the paneling. It felt … hollow.

The murmuring stopped.

Aggravated, Elsyn pushed hard on the wall. It gave—no, it *rolled* away from her, the boards holding the tureens detaching neatly from the shelving on either side of it. It was a floor-to-ceiling cabinet, wheels hidden by the skirting. It swung back into another hallway that continued out of the scullery.

Neddie stood there, face schooled into her very blandest expression. Elsyn would make two of her, she thought irritably; she was not much more than a bundle of dry bones. Next to the accountant stood a person wearing the blue livery of a servant and a cloth wrapped around their head, a perfectly unremarkable person, slender, with knobby wrists and a thin, fox-like face—

"*You*," Elsyn said to the High Priest, equal measures bewildered, angry, and relieved. "You're dead! She had you—well, she said you were dead, anyway!" After the livestock plague, the High Priest had ever-so-diplomatically suggested that some royal resources might be sent to local temples helping with the efforts to clear the dead animals. The following evening, the false Taryn had announced that they had been taken violently ill in the night and sent to see her own personal doctor in the countryside. Everyone had known what that meant. The royal family had never, to anyone's knowledge, had a personal doctor in the countryside.

"Maybe less dead than previously thought to be the case," the High Priest said.

"It's been *a year*," Elsyn went on. She heard her own voice crack and forcibly lowered it. "Where have you *been* all that time?"

"Well," the High Priest said, gesturing to the livery. "The qu—Ta —she wasn't the sort of person to look closely at someone washing dishes."

"But other people are," Elsyn hissed. "How did none of her favorites catch you? Eradelior?" Neddie blanched at the mention of the false Taryn's special favorite, who had been found dead in a closet the day after the fairy queen had been killed. "Any of them? Did she appoint no one to make sure you actually vanished?"

The High Priest and Neddie exchanged a look.

"Did you use magic?" Elsyn snapped. She wanted to yank her own hair out. Priests were theoretically above misdirections and charms, glamours and ill-wishings, even when they were away from the magic-negating properties of the temples. At least, she thought sourly, so she had been told as an initiate.

"Well," Neddie said.

"Well," the high priest said. "Not *only* magic."

That was too much. "You knew, then," Elsyn said. "You *knew* she was a fake. A changeling. A *fairy*. You had to have seen it, if you knew magic at all. And you did nothing to stop her or—or—" She tried to bite off the sentence, but it kept going without her "—or help me." She took a deep breath. "You *let* her arrange their deaths, you *let* her be crowned, you let her—"

"I think you overestimate my abilities," the High Priest said. Their voice was quiet, but it filled up the room. Neddie's facial expression had gone past blankness into porcelain chamber pot territory.

"I've been queen for three weeks. I've no friends and no allies in this city," Elsyn said. "I'm your priest. You're obligated to me, by word and by vow. I'm your queen. You're obligated to me, by—by blood, by birth. She's been gone for five weeks. You've had *five weeks* to tell me you were still alive, still doing—" She gestured expansively about the secret hallway. "—*whatever* you're doing, and you didn't."

The silence in the hallway was suddenly deafening. Elsyn realized there were tears in her eyes and tears on her cheeks.

Maybe being married would not be so awful, she thought, if it meant she wouldn't be *alone* all the time.

"We thought we'd be able to get the real Taryn back," Neddie blurted. "From whichever fairy had taken her. We thought we could put things back to normal."

"The real Taryn is gone," Elsyn said, biting off each word. She thought fleetingly, bitterly of her last glimpse of her actual, flesh-and-blood sister, standing against the far wall of throne room, between the shadow of her goblin king and her forest witch as she watched Elsyn be crowned. All three of them had vanished before the ceremony had concluded. *She* had been able to flee this disaster, leaving Elsyn to face a kingdom of enemies alone. "I am the only queen you have left."

The witan consisted of twelve very large goblins who definitely did not smell like any family Kandar knew. They smelled like limestone, not granite, and salt, not horses. All of them wore the same sort of silver jewelry, and dull tunics, where the court of his king preferred eye-blistering color. Otherwise he would not have known them for strangers; their ears, eyes, tusks, and tails were familiar shapes and their crests a familiar range of hues. Goblin blood, even when mixed with fairy or human, tended to win out. Usdar, his mother, had been a human, though a different sort of human who had come from another time, one could speak to stones and smell the gods' footsteps. Kandar looked nothing like her, and he had often regretted this.

Elsyn could probably smell the gods' footsteps, he thought.

The witan stood around him in the short green grass. Behind them rose a ring of white standing stones, and behind the rocks a crowd of other goblins gawked and muttered to each other. Most were armed with spears and halberds. The young goblin Telred had been given the duty of watching Socks. Kandar couldn't see either of them, and he hoped they weren't getting into mischief.

But where did they all *come* from? he thought, staring around. *We're* the only ones left! That's the whole story, why the king's father welcomed the horse-lords and their queen! I've never heard of any others —any more of *us*.

"I am Telwulf, the leader of the moot," the tallest member of the witan said. She stepped forward, a female goblin with tusks as thick as Kandar's wrists. In the normal way of things, he would have liked to tussle with her; she was very handsome indeed. "What brings you here, Kandar of the house of Haldar?"

"Kandar of the house of Haldar, foster brother to the king of goblins," he corrected.

The thick-tusked goblin narrowed her eyes at him. "What right have you to walk the goblin road?" she asked crisply.

No mention of Albenyssar. Kandar would have given the same response he had given before, only more loudly and with more extravagant rudeness, if Socks had not suddenly whinnied at an ear-splitting volume from somewhere beyond the standing stones.

Hello! Hello! You are a human! You smell like a horse. Do you have snacks? Where is your horse? I would like to say hello. I would like to eat snacks and then say hello. Where are your snacks?

A low, resonant laugh floated above the crowd. It did not sound like a goblin's laugh.

"Excuse me, I have to see to my horse," Kandar said, diving between the two closest members of the witan.

They yelled and tried to block him with their pole-arms, but he was still faster, twisting and leaping to the top of a standing stone. From there he could see Socks, who had freed himself from the hapless Telred. Kandar launched himself again, clearing seven pairs of pointed goblin ears and at least as many spear-tips, before landing on his horse's back.

Socks stamped one of his front feet. You are *interrupting*, he complained, before immediately going on, This is my new friend Ben. He's going to give me food. Perhaps oats, he added suggestively.

Kandar peered down from his seat, both discomfited and intrigued.

Ben was a young man, almost as young as Elsyn. The noble families of her country were clearly cut from the same cloth; his heavy black brows, arched nose, and large dark eyes reminded Kandar of the queen. His jaw was square, covered in a short beard that did not entirely obscure a deep dimple in his left cheek.

He was also, for a human, enormous. Kandar was certainly taller —he could push himself up on his tail if there was any contest—but Albenyssar was half again as wide through the shoulders, barrel-chested, barrel-bellied, with great stout legs. Elsyn would look normal-sized next to him, as would the tremendous holy cattle.

"I'm going to nail your ears to a rock," Telwulf said from behind him. "Ben, Telgol was supposed to tell you that someone was looking for you and to lie low."

"She did," Ben said. "That's why I came up to see who it was."

"Stupid man," Telwulf said, but without venom.

"Yes," Ben said. "But no surprise there." He had been vigorously scratching Socks behind the jaw, but now he looked up at Kandar. "I'm surprised a goblin would want anything to do with Her Majesty the Queen," he said, bitterness creeping into his voice. "All goblins I have met are honorable folk."

Kandar was surprised by the surge of protective irritation that rose in his chest. "I am honored to serve the Queen Elsyn," he said coldly.

Ben's face went still. "Elsyn?" he repeated. "Elsyn?"

Of course he doesn't know, Kandar thought belatedly. No news makes its way up the goblin road. "Taryn is no longer the queen," he said, wondering how much he ought to explain. "Elsyn was crowned four weeks past."

"Crowned," Ben repeated. "But Elsyn is—Elsyn is a priest. She can't—she doesn't—"

"And now she is Priest-Queen, the first in all history," said Kandar. "Or so I am told."

Socks, bored with their conversation, bumped Ben with his nose. Hello hello, have you considered that you have stopped giving scratches, and that is very inconvenient, he said.

Ben mechanically reached up to rub along the horse's withers. Can he hear Socks, Kandar wondered, or does he just know horses? His hands were wide and brown, with well-formed nails. A thin white line ran across the knuckles of his left one. "She'll have the help of the temple, at least," he muttered. He didn't seem to be talking to anyone in particular. "Even if —well." He shook himself. His eyes had gone a little wild, but he squared his shoulders and turned his face up to the goblin. "Thank you for the news, but you needn't have come all this way. I am of no importance to any queen, past or present. Give Elsyn—give Her Majesty—she has my fondest—I wish her the very—"

"She sent me to bring you back to her," Kandar cut in. He had meant to say "the capital," or "into the land of men," or even "her service," but the effect of the word he did choose was stunning and immediate. All the blood drained out of Ben's face. The hand he had been using to caress Socks fell limply to his side.

"She can't want me there now," he said flatly. "Not—no. She could not." He stared up at Kandar, his eyes unseeing.

"This is all very interesting," Telwulf said from behind them both. Two of the witan, wiry female goblins carrying silver-banded spears, elbowed themselves in front of Socks. "Ben, I'm not sending you anywhere on the strength of some woman's word."

"She's not *some woman*," Ben said, rousing himself. Kandar looked at him approvingly; at least they were of an accord about one thing. "Elsyn—Her Majesty—the woman who is now queen was once—a friend. A childhood friend. Though it has been a long time."

"Nevertheless," Telwulf went on, striding up to stand between the spear-wielders. She glared at Kandar in a distinctively protective manner. "There's no sense in you charging about with no information and no preparation. We'll sit and have beer and some cheese and decide what is to be done."

"Very well," Kandar said.

"Very well," Ben echoed.

Ben found he couldn't taste the cheese or the beer. Telden had cut him an enormous piece of the former, and Telfar had filled him what looked like a small cauldron of the latter, but he chewed and drank automatically.

Elsyn was queen, he thought. Elsyn was queen. Had he ever imagined she might be? Had she?

In the before-times, when whatever had happened to make Taryn into a monster had not yet happened, Elsyn had been shy and awkward. She had been afraid of new people. He and Taryn—oh, Two-Bodied God, there was a thought! He and Taryn had once been friends, too!—had taken turns standing up for her. Taryn had always been forceful, even as a small, deceptively delicate-looking child, good at bullying adults who wished to seek favor with the royal family. He had not had the same self-assurance, but it had been easy to stand in front of Elsyn and tell people off, particularly the sorts of nobles who thought they could play the sisters off one another. Most especially it had been easy when other noble children had called her fat or slow or any of the other horrible things they had heard their mothers say. They had done their best to separate Elsyn from her sister, to belittle her and weaken Taryn.

It had been easy to protect Elsyn. He took another bite of the cheese, but it was hard to swallow.

The goblin tribe sat, stood, or draped themselves over an array of trestle tables set up in the hollow on the leeward side of the caves. They each had a hunk of cheese, and someone had pulled out a jar of salt fish and was passing it around. The goats had mostly been penned up, though several yearlings had escaped and were now trying to steal the fish off the tables. A storm was blowing in off the wyrd-worm sea, and Telwulf had decided they ought to get some fresh air before they were trapped inside for all of tomorrow.

The goblin Kandar sat on a large rock, a little apart from the rest. His stallion, after determining that he would not be allowed to have any cheese, beer, or fish, had wandered up the hill to greet Quince where he grazed. When Ben glanced up at them, the other horse was trying to entice his elderly dun gelding to play a game of chase. Quince only flicked his ears, bemused. He would put himself away in a straw-filled cave, kept spotlessly clean for him by various goblin children, before the rain started. Ben hoped the other horse had the good sense to follow him.

Kandar's large orange eyes were trained on Ben. He had made no pretense he was not staring throughout dinner. Periodically his long tail lashed. Ben wondered what he was thinking, and whether he was telling the truth. Had Elsyn really sent him? If she had, what did that mean? Did she trust this goblin? What had happened to Taryn? Had this fellow had something to do with it?

He was, as goblins and humans went, very fine-looking, with lovely long limbs and a beautifully shaped face. His hands tended toward the elegant. Ben noticed Teljur and Tielen giving him thoughtful, interested looks. He smiled a bit at that, in spite of everything; Kandar would need a week to recover between the two of them.

Tielen caught him looking and grinned a big, toothy grin, which Ben reluctantly returned.

What would it be like, to go among other humans again? He had ridden the goblin road out of his own world seven years ago, despairing, exhausted, heartbroken. He had not expected to ever go home. He had not expected to ever see his mother or Elsyn or any of the other people he had so badly disappointed again.

But then, Ben had not thought he would survive his first encounter with the goblins, either. He hadn't expected goblins at all, but a monster which couldn't be properly named or described. He'd been sent on a mission he had no hope of returning from, and that hadn't seemed like the worst thing. At least it would have been an end to the shame. Except—the goblins hadn't killed him, and for all Telwulf's grumbling, they'd never really considered it. There had been no monster at all.

"Look like you could use some more beer," Tielen yelled at him, and another bowl was slotted into his hands.

His head had gone muzzy, and the fact that he'd already finished the little cauldron's worth of drink surprised him. Maybe it was a good thing. The alcohol made the echoes of loneliness and grief seem farther away, duller.

If he believed Kandar, Ben might see Elsyn again.

He set the bowl down on the trestle table with a clunk and stood up.

"Much honor to you, my lady," he said called across the tables to Telwulf. "I fear I must retire for the evening."

"Are you—" she started to ask, but he'd already untangled himself from the bench and was walking back toward the caves.

Kandar watched Ben get to his feet and leave the dinner. He noticed how, even inebriated, the man moved with careful grace, easing his bulk through the gathered goblins without jostling elbows or stepping on tails. He noticed, too, that Ben's shoulder was slapped again and again, and several hands grabbed his and shook them enthusiastically. The goblins did not want him to go to bed early. Ben bent his head to anyone who addressed him, responding with a murmur or a wry grin.

Several thoughts tangled themselves up in Kandar's head. He

wanted to follow Ben and talk to him. There was something unpleasant buried here, something that had to do with Elsyn and the false queen before her, and he ought to find out what it was. He needed to convince Ben to come back to the capital city. Besides all that, Ben might be willing to tell Kandar what he had learned of these new goblins, who even the goblin king had not known of—

Watching Ben walk was very like watching Elsyn move among her cattle. They were, each of them, mesmerizing.

The air had gone cool and blue around the raucous company. A white flash threw shadows across the trestles, and a crack followed a second later. The chatter and laughter changed tenor, as bowls were stacked, cheese was wrapped up, and the tables were disassembled. The shadowing clouds let loose the first salvo of rain.

Kandar slipped down from the rock where he sat and ran after Ben.

He had gone round the hill, past the main entrance to the goblin caves, and down the path that went to the sea. Kandar had nosed down that way earlier, before a heavily-armed goblin carrying a basket of fish up the hill had offered him an unsheathed knife and her bared tusks. The path cut down through the hill into a deep, grassy crevasse. The glint of silver water was barely visible at the bottom.

Ben disappeared behind a stone set into the steep bank. Kandar, unthinking, followed him.

The tall stone marked a limestone vestibule, at the back of which was a door made of driftwood. It was cracked open, though there was no light in the chamber beyond. It was not a large room; he could hear Ben's movements from where he stood.

Kandar shouldered through the door.

Goblin eyes were first made to see in the dark. The cave was small, a single room, with an unlit brazier in one corner and a small table in another, across from a low bed against the wall. Ben sat on the edge of the thin mattress, leaning forward, his elbows on his knees, head lifted.

Kandar stepped forward and crouched in front of him, bringing his face a hand's-breadth from Ben's. Now, he thought, I should start with some niceties. Perhaps chat about the weather.

"Who were you to Elsyn?" he asked. Who are you going to be to Elsyn? he wanted to add.

Ben took a deep breath and let it go through his nose. "I am no one in particular."

"You're lying."

"Deragcaish is a ducal house and very close to the royal one. My mother was part of her mother's retinue. I was often in the palace as a child."

Kandar sniffed the air. Ben's scent filled the air, a warm human smell overlaid with horse and beer and salt. It was a good smell. Probably Ben would take it the wrong way if Kandar jammed his nose into his armpit. Or maybe he would take it the right way. "You're still lying. Your queen didn't send me across an ocean of grass and up a goblin road for a man she knew incidentally."

He noted the shudder that went through Ben's body at the words *your queen.* He resolved to use them as often as possible.

"It's none of your business," he said.

"It will be my business," Kandar said. "I am going to marry Elsyn."

Ben went still. The faint gleam of his eyes fell into shadow.

Kandar fought an absurd impulse to—what? Not to defend his right to marry a queen. He felt no qualms about the nobility of his mother's bloodline, even if he was not its finest representative. He didn't feel his decision to offer for her, nor his certainty that Elsyn would choose him, needed explanation—both were self-evident.

No, he wanted to say something like: *It will be all right,* or worse yet: *Trust me.*

Ben cleared his throat, and his voice was thick when he finally spoke. "So you left El—forgive me, your *affianced*—alone, in that hell-hole, that pit of vipers—to come here—"

"I did not," Kandar broke in. "Ildar, the wizard of the goblin court, and three dozen of my kinsfolk are with her. Your human kingdom has never seen finer warriors or minds more clever. And you left her too, didn't you?" The room had grown so dark even he could not make out the shadows anymore; a cloud must have gone across the moon. He wanted to touch Ben's face, to feel what expression he was making.

"My being there made things worse," Ben said dully. "And then, after—after I dishonored myself, I would have only been a tool for Taryn to use against her."

"Dishonored yourself? Dishonored." Kandar repeated the word, tasting it. It was sour. "How?"

Ben let out a bark of laughter. "Why should the worst moments of my life be yours for the hearing, son of Haldar?"

"If you stay here, it won't matter what I know. I will become— nothing, a story your goblins tell themselves on rainy days. No human will

follow me back here. I would not betray the knowledge of a goblin road."
He inched closer, until he could feel Ben's shallow breaths stir the fur on
his face. "If you come back with me, you must become a new man in
service of your queen. A new man with no secrets and no shame." It took
a great deal of effort to keep his voice low and even. He felt like storming,
like shouting. "In which case, you would have to shake free of it—
whatever it is—anyhow."

"You ask a great deal," Ben said. His voice was so soft that
Kandar, close as he was, could not feel the air leave his lips. "I doubt you
know how much."

"A great deal is needed," Kandar said, unsure. What had Ben
done? He felt more and more certain that Elsyn loved this man, or had
loved him. The sea-goblins clearly respected and cared for him. Socks
liked him, and Socks, incorrigible as he was, judged character impeccably.
How badly had Ben erred? Was restoring his honor within the powers of
goblin prince, even one as tenacious as himself?

Ben drew back from him. The bed creaked under his substantial
weight.

"Let me sleep on it," he said. He suddenly sounded as tired as
death. "I still have a bit of pride left, and I would like to tell the story
properly."

Kandar got to his feet stiffly. He did not want to leave. He
wanted, if he were being perfectly honest with himself, to shove his face
under Ben's bearded jaw and breathe in the smell of his skin, and then
follow a number of other vague whims that he was sure would solidify
with a bit of exploration. He wondered, suddenly, if Elsyn dreamed of
Ben, and if she dreamed of some of the same things he was thinking now.

He bowed in the darkness.

"Good night, Albenyssar of Deragcaish," he said and left the
chamber under the hill.

Elsyn, lying on the floor of the temple barn, did not dream. She
lay awake in the straw, staring at the ancient rafters far overhead. Around
her, the cows lowed. Turnip and Onion were particularly worried about
her. Every so often a large, wet nose appeared in her field of vision to
sniff her, and a long, purple tongue explored her face. Her hair was stiff
with cow saliva.

Periodically she fell into a doze and then started awake, unable to remember why she was neither in the priests' dormitory nor in the royal chambers. Those rooms had been cleaned of the false Taryn's possessions shortly before the coronation. What had definitely belonged to the fairy impostor—dresses, jewelry, small unpleasant knickknacks—she had ordered burned. Then, when the servants had refused to touch any of it, she had crammed all of the brick-a-brac and clothes into boxes and carried them to the pasture with three of the younger priests.

The bonfire they had built had sputtered and sparked with sickly colors, and she had thought some nasty little spell might have loosed itself back into the palace, had the herd not gathered around the flames, their horns making a fence from which nothing escaped. The heirlooms—the massive bed where most of her ancestors had been conceived and birthed, a few of the larger jewels, the tapestries depicting the battles fought by her grandfather and her great-grandmother—she could not burn, though they were itchy with a thin film of magic. Elsyn could not bear to touch any of it. She could not sleep in or even look at that bed for too long, and many nights she slept in one of the closets that had been used only for the queen's special linens, now empty.

None of that answered the question of why she was lying on the cold stone floor of the barn. Her lower back ached. Light angled low across the dusty wall near her face; the sun must be setting soon. Her arms, uncovered by her priest's shift, prickled with cold. A piece of straw was jabbing her in the neck.

Elsyn sat up.

Parsnip's calf was not yet old enough to have a name, but she gave Elsyn's face a sniff.

"Good evening, little one," she whispered. Her head swam. The back of her skull pounded.

NOT A GOOD EVENING. There was Bean. TERRIBLE EVENING. STUPID EVENING. STUPID EVENING WITH STUPID PEOPLE.

"What happened?" Elsyn asked. She swallowed hard; her stomach lurched unpleasantly.

ATTACK, Bean said. STUPID. Her tail slapped against her back.

Elsyn brought a hand to her head. Her fingers found a sticky lump just behind her ear.

"Oh," she said, her heart sinking.

She thought she had been out in the city with—had she been with Neddie? Yes, it had been Neddie. She had said there was a group of

priests who would like to talk to her, and she had gone to meet them—
they had left the palace late last night, by a side door, dressed in dark, plain
clothes—

Obviously something had gone wrong. The next thought came
before she could stop it: this was just the time it would be nice to have a
husband—perhaps a tall, dark one, who could move through the shadows
invisibly, only a flash of orange eyes occasionally revealing his presence—
to watch her back. Or, indeed, a friend. But it had been a long time since
Ben had stood between her and a bully. "Bean, did you rescue me?"

TURNIP, Bean said. VERY FAST.

Modesty is not considered a virtue by cows. Turnip licked Elsyn's
face again, smugness in every line of her great body.

"You are a good sister, Turnip," she said, pressing her forehead
against the cow's cheek.

Turnip agreed with this statement.

"Where did you rescue me from?" Elsyn asked, carefully getting
to her feet. Her head throbbed.

Turnip's notions of direction were largely confined to the temple
and its pastures, and the place where she had charged Elsyn's attackers was
neither of those. The cow had been able to swing her head, so not a tight
alley. Based on the shadowy memory she shared of hallways with
discolored grass growing over the walls and floors (carpets and tapestries,
Elsyn inferred), she had left the temple complex by sneaking through the
palace.

Elsyn briefly considered the image of a seven-foot-tall cow
sneaking.

STREET, Bean suggested. OUTSIDE. MANY STUPID
PEOPLE.

That part of the memory was even more unclear. Turnip mostly
remembered smells; the comforting, almost-bovine smell of Elsyn and the
odd, papery scent of the accountant Neddie, suddenly joined by the
unpleasant tang of unfamiliar human sweat and metal. There had been at
least two attackers. Turnip had suddenly been there, swinging her great
head and bellowing. One man had run, making a horrible noise like a
carrion crow.

"How did you know you needed to come get me?" A horrible
understanding came upon her. "Turnip, did you follow me?"

DON'T HAVE TO FOLLOW IF COW STAYS WITH HERD,
Bean said reproachfully.

The lump on her head sent a sharp twinge through her skull. She buried her face against Bean's smooth, warm hide. "I don't know how I'm going to rule a kingdom from behind a line of cows," she mumbled. What had happened? Had Neddie led her into an ambush? Had she betrayed Elsyn, or had she been betrayed?

Why had Elsyn thought it was a good idea to follow Neddie into dark streets? she wondered, until she remembered with a sinking feeling in the pit of her stomach. Neddie had given her a name she trusted, even after all this time. It looked like she had been wrong to do so.

"How did you get me back?"

Turnip didn't think Elsyn had been completely unconscious; she'd put both arms around the cow's neck and stumbled next to her for a long time. A long, nightmarish sequence, of walking and falling and getting up again, coalesced in Elsyn's memory. She pushed it away.

Was this an attempt at kidnapping, or assassination? Elsyn supposed there were a half-dozen noble families who'd like to see her married off to one of their most biddable sons. The Glascrann, the lesser branch of Deragcaish, the Keevnar, and ... she couldn't remember any more. And then, once there was a child, there was no reason to keep her around.

Even that might be too generous, she thought, her heart pounding faster. Plenty of those same noble families were related by some degree of cousinhood to the royal line. Family trees could be doctored to give someone a better claim, if marrying the living queen didn't seem like a good proposition.

"Probably the only reason no one has tried to kill me before this is because I'm surrounded by holy cows," she went on, mostly to herself.

NO ONE FIGHTS THE HERD, Bean responded. Turnip, Parsley, and Parsley's calf agreed with her.

Elsyn stroked a dappled patch on Bean's shoulder, steadying herself. A different emotion crept up in her throat, one that she had shoved back relentlessly as a frightened thirteen-year-old left to the temple, unwanted by her parents, mocked by her court, undefended by her sister. Not fear, but *rage*.

She tugged at her white shift, smoothing the thick linen over her belly and her hips. Her hand passed over a small, hard object stuck inside the fabric. She drew out the pouch she wore tied at her waist under her clothes. The tiny knife Jolar had given her was still inside.

She was queen now. Priest-queen, anointed of the Two-Bodied God, member of the sacred herd. She did not have to push down her rage.

But neither could she afford to be foolish. Someone, and most likely several dozen someones, actively wished her ill, and the only allies she could be sure of also had hooves and horns. She would have to try another angle to get in contact with the surviving priests, this time better prepared and defended. She did not fully trust that the goblin king did not intend to manipulate her for his own ends, but at least the goblins hadn't tried to kill her yet. A public association with them might discourage anyone else from trying.

And, if Kandar returned with Ben—which, she told her hastily, he would not—but if he *did,* she would have already made a courteous overture to his people. Useful for someone you might marry.

"Turnip, will you accompany me on another trip into the city?" she asked, holding out her hand to the cow.

Turnip considered, swishing her tail, before licking her palm.

THE HERD STICKS TOGETHER, Bean said firmly. WE GO.

The sea-goblins ate dried fish for breakfast, a barbaric practice Kandar wished the laws of hospitality allowed him to rebuke. As the rain pounded down outside the cave, they handed around mugs of steaming herbal tea and a plate of hard, white, salty bricks. Each sleepy goblin took a brick and dipped it in a mug to soften it, filling the air with a smell stronger than a mare birthing inside a tent. Telred, when they noticed Kandar's facial expression, offered him a large jar of unidentifiable pickled vegetables to eat on top of his fish.

Ben was nowhere to be seen. Kandar supposed he was still hiding in his limestone burrow.

Hello why haven't you come out to see me yet, came Socks' plaintive voice through the stone wall. I've only been given a cup of grain and four lumps of hay. It's a very small cup. Can I share your breakfast? I've just run out of things to eat and Quince doesn't want to share. Quince is very mean.

A much softer voice murmured, Quince is very patient.

"Excuse me," Kandar said, bouncing to his feet. He bowed to Telwulf. "My horse is being rude. I have to go rescue him from himself."

Telwulf's skeptical eyebrows followed him, as he vaulted over a trestle table and ducked outside.

Ropes of water lashed down over his head and shoulders, and he squinted at the horizon. Curtains of rain hid the glimmer of the sea. It felt as if air, land, and ocean had become one soggy mass of gray reaching in all directions.

The horse-cave was in the opposite direction from Ben's chamber, just the other side of the great goblin hill. How far did these goblin lands go? he wondered. What lay past their boundaries? The goblin kingdom in the mountains-just-to-the-left bordered on haunted marshes, and beyond them, dark woods. Doors among those trees opened into any number of worlds. The mountains themselves went on for a very long time, populated in their farthest reaches by dragons and herds of goat-like unicorns with long beards and tiny hooves. Beyond that, a vague gray plain unfolded above and just to the left of the human kingdom, but it wasn't very real, and goblins rarely went there. Had the sea-goblins crossed that plain to come to this place?

Lost in thought, he jerked when Socks stretched his neck out of a cave entrance and nipped at his tunic. I thought you were never coming, he told Kandar, in tragic tones. I thought I was going to starve.

"Don't feed him any more," came Ben's voice from inside the cave. "If he says he hasn't eaten, he's lying."

Kandar shoved Socks back. "You'll catch a chill."

The inside of the horse-cave was surprisingly dry. Someone—the sea-goblins? Ben?—had built a large, conical ceramic stove in the center of the space, the chimney joining the ceiling. Kandar nervously laid a hand on the surface—Socks was not the most careful of horses—but it was only pleasantly warm, not hot. Quince stood dozing with his rump toward the heat, one foot lifted. A gray blanket draped his body. Ben knelt by the stove's small arched mouth, feeding it dried black bricks of earth.

He gestured. "There's a board to block the wind."

Kandar set the board in place and crouched by Ben.

"It's a good stove," he said, watching the flicker of fire light the stubble covering Ben's jaw. He had shaved off most of his beard this morning. He still had a very nice jaw.

"Telfar helped me build it," Ben said, sounding absent. "It rains so much here, I worried about hoof rot if Quince couldn't dry out properly."

Kandar considered this. "How long ago was that?"

Ben was silent for a minute. Socks made a little noise, wanting to interrupt, but Kandar shushed him.

"A few months after I arrived here," he said. "Nearly seven years ago."

So he had known very early on that he would not be returning to the other humans, Kandar thought. Questions itched at him, but he did not know which, if any, Ben would answer.

One in particular was too difficult to keep inside. "Who are you to Elsyn?" he asked once more. It sounded as though he were jealous. He was jealous, of some shared, unknowable history, of some past trust.

"We are cousins, of a sort," Ben said slowly. He rocked back on his heels. "Both of us are descended from a king who ruled a century or two ago. Her line continued on the throne, and mine established a ducal house. I suppose that is not what you are asking."

"No." Kandar waited.

Ben stared at the pile of dried fuel.

"Our mothers—I suppose it started there. I was always in the palace, from a very young age. The house of Deragcaish—after the royal family themselves, there is no one of higher rank. I suppose the queen wanted to keep my mother close." He paused, staring down at his hands resting on his thighs. "It seems unbelievable now—after everything—but we—the girls and I—were friends. Good friends. We were close enough in age. We had games, and stories that no one else knew that we told each other. I was not—I was not welcome, among the other noble children. Taryn was kind, as a child, and Elsyn needed me." His voice was so tightly controlled that it betrayed his anguish as surely as if it had broken.

Elsyn still needs you, Kandar thought but did not say. "Then why —"

Ben let out a gasp of desperately unhappy laughter. "I am an idiot, and everyone who loves me has paid for it." The words came more and more quickly, as though he could not wait any longer to rid himself of something poisonous. "You must understand this. You must understand why I cannot go back—why I'm no good to Elsyn now. There was a young man. He was an envoy, newly arrived from a country far away. He was—he was very charming, and very—I thought he liked me. There were several weeks, when we—when we were rarely apart. I thought—" His face was turned toward the wall now, but his fingers dug into the fabric of his trousers. "I would have never been so—so enamored—if he had not shown, in every way, that he desired my company—"

Kandar felt his stomach sink.

"He approached my mother first. He said—he said that I had forced him into a relationship. He was alone and young in a strange land, and when I showed interest in him, he had not felt able to refuse. He told her I had—I had made him do things he would not have chosen to do."

"But—" Kandar started. Every additional detail of this story made the fur on his shoulders and back stiffen.

"My mother is an honorable woman, from an honorable house," Ben went on, sounding sick. "She wanted nothing to do with any person who would so abuse the trust of a subordinate. She drew up papers of disownment." He took a deep breath. "And then the envoy disappeared. I did not—I swear to any god who will listen that I did not lay a hand upon him. I didn't see him, for a week before they pulled the body out of a gutter."

Oh, no, Kandar thought. This is several layers more muck than I was expecting.

"What was my mother to think? What was anyone to think? Word got out, about what kind of person I really was. There should have been a trial." His voice was as bitter as bile. "Tary—the *queen*—gave my mother the great kindness of sending me away to kill the dragon Ibirgordion, so I could vanish instead of being hanged. Ibirgordion—who had not been seen by human eyes for a thousand years. But leaving as quietly as possible was the only thing left for me. I could not bear to shame my family, or—or anyone else I loved, more than I already had."

Suddenly Socks stamped his foot. I have been quiet for hours and hours and hours, he said. He lipped Ben's face and hair. This story is boring. Give me more food.

Kandar shook his head, as if that would clear the flood of nonsense out of his skull.

"You were set up," he said.

Turnip was a very stealthy creature. Elsyn had known that an unusual amount of produce went missing when the white-dappled cow was about the temple kitchens, but the barely-suppressed exclamations of surprise from her goblin companions made it clear that most large animals of their acquaintance did not move quite so delicately through city streets. Watching her disappear into another splinter of shadow, it occurred to Elsyn that some cows might be competent magic-users.

Bean was not stealthy at all. She strolled across wide thoroughfares and stopped in front of shop doors, forcing wagons, riders, and pedestrians alike to wait for her. Humans yelled and threw curses, but no ox, mule, or horse would dare challenge the Boss Cow.

Elsyn and two goblins moved unobserved through the chaos of her wake. When she had arrived at their guest quarters in the lower palace —the side doors and windows of which had been barricaded, she noticed uneasily—only Jolar and an unknown goblin, introduced as Amlar, had been present. Jolar had listened to her edited story politely, but she had offered no information about where the other goblins had gone.

I have received news of a group of priests who are in hiding, Elsyn repeated to herself. I believe they may have information of use to both of us. She knew where Neddie had meant to take her, and she didn't want to find out alone if she had been telling the truth about the surviving priests. She had not mentioned the attack to the goblins, and she did not explain why Bean and Turnip accompanied her. She hoped the hood of her cloak hid the bump on the side of her head.

Her story of why the priests asked for a meeting continued: The temple of the Two-Bodied God had once had substantial holdings bordering the goblin road. Though the path itself was mostly invisible, occasionally nucklavees and other strange beasts jumped from the road into temple fields and terrorized their livestock. Many of those pastures had been abandoned after the false Taryn had been crowned, because she refused to send soldiers to defend the boundary temples. Maybe the goblins could do something on their end of the road, and those fields could once again be used for pasture or cultivation.

The truth—that she might be walking into the house of someone who had just tried to murder her, and she didn't want to do it alone—felt impossible to utter. The longer she thought about the attack two nights before, the more wobbly and frightened she felt. It would have been so easy to hit her a little harder, with something a little sharper, and then the cows would be completely on their own.

She thought Bean and Turnip could protect her. She hoped she could protect them.

Turnip led them through the dairy district, where she suspected that both of the cows were getting news from other local ungulates, then the produce district and the street of flower-sellers. Bean stole a large bouquet of pink damask roses, and a very small man with a very large black mustache shook his fist at her. She swung her great head in his direction and pawed the ground, and he hid behind a stand of sunflowers.

They crept up a smaller street, this one occupied by gold- and silversmiths. It was harder for the goblins to pass unnoticed here, and after a polite nod both Jolar and Amlar disappeared upward, scaling the side of a stone house like a ladder. Elsyn could see two shadows passing from roof to roof out of the corner of her eye. She pulled her cloak closer around her face. She had not been seen outside the palace in the past ten years, but she looked so much like Taryn that it would not be hard to identify her. Now she walked in front of Bean, who was having a fine time eating window box flowers and nosing over display boards in front of shops.

Elsyn recognized the neighborhood Turnip had led them to with a jolt. There were two noble districts in the city. The newer one had been built in the last two generations on the alluvial plain at the outskirts. The flat terrain allowed the great families to build sprawling mansions with multiple wings and luxurious gardens. The older district, nearly as old as the palace and temple themselves, dated from a time when noble houses needed to be fortified. It had grown up on a narrow hilltop that faced the palatial hill. This was the slope they were climbing now, up a narrowing street that switched back on itself again and again.

She had once spent a great deal of time in one of these houses.

Many of these older mansions did not have windows facing the street, and only the flutter of greenery over the parapets above gave any hint that people still lived here. It felt like climbing through a canyon, Elsyn thought, her heart pounding.

The street opened into a small courtyard at the top of the noble hill. Five high stone houses encircled the open space, their facades making a claustrophobic cylinder around a fountain. A white stone serpent curved upward from the surface of the water and spat a crystalline arc of liquid back into the basin.

Elsyn's heart felt like it would claw its way out of her chest.

She glanced upward. Two shadows like gargoyles sat on the edge of the roof behind her, waiting. Turnip stood in the shadow of the horse gate of one of the houses, remarkably inconspicuous. Elsyn could no longer hear the heavy tread of Bean's hooves a few yards behind her.

She took a deep breath and stepped forward.

The portal directly in front of her, massive and heavily carved with twined heraldic symbols, crowned by an archway of stone beasts, creaked ominously. A much smaller door cut into its surface opened, and a woman stepped out into the courtyard.

She was very tall and broad-shouldered, wearing a long coat in Deragcaish red. A chignon at the base of her neck contained her shining black hair, heavily streaked with silver. She regarded Elsyn for a long time with a face that was painfully familiar. Her expression was as cold as death.

"Elsyn," Ben's mother said finally. "Your Majesty the Queen." She tilted her head, the barest hint of acknowledgment.

"Set up?" Ben said blankly.

He had not been able to look at Kandar while he told the story. Seven years later, the thought of his utter failure, and the shocked disappointment and despair in his mother's face, still made his whole body rigid with pain.

Telwulf and the other goblins knew only the barest outline of his final weeks in the capital city. He had told her he had been sentenced to seek the dragon Ibirgordion as punishment for a crime. She had never asked for details, and he had not tried to find out more information about whether the dragon had ever passed through goblin lands, or if it had ever existed at all.

He glanced up. The reddish glow from the stove reflected in the goblin's orange eyes. Cloud-misted white light leaked around the board blocking the doorway and made the tips of his crest glow. It was not that the goblins of the sea weren't fine creatures in their own right, he found himself thinking. But none of them had the same intensity, like lightning sparking from every gesture and facial expression, as Kandar did.

"What do you mean, set up?" he repeated, feeling slow and stupid.

"How far away was this country that sent the envoy?"

Ben rubbed his face. "There are partly independent baronies in the south of the kingdom."

"Is that what he said?"

Ben suddenly felt itchy both inside and outside. "He might have been from beyond the great southern sea."

"Did he speak with an accent?"

"No. Perhaps he was a magic user. I have heard of such things, charms which allow the learning of languages—"

"Did he ever speak to you of this charm?"

"We did not—ah—spend so much time talking—"

Kandar interrupted. "Who identified the body?"

"Palace officials—"

"Did you get a look at it?"

Ben felt heat creeping across his face and his throat tightening. "*His body*," he forced out from between his teeth, "had been submerged for some time. I couldn't see much, but there were certain—identifying marks. A particular necklace. Two moles on his left shoulder."

"Were there clear marks of his having been murdered?"

"You're a right gentleman," Ben snapped.

Kandar clicked his tongue behind his teeth impatiently. "And you're a fool if you can't see what I'm getting at. I'm trying to help you. Were there marks?"

Ben felt another long-suppressed wave of nausea come over him, and the need to have the truth out of his body temporarily overpowered his anger at the goblin's presumption. "There was a rope," he said quietly. "Around his neck. Given everything—well, I thought he had probably done it himself. But—there's hardly a space between that and me killing him."

"There's a space farther than Socks could cover in a day's hard gallop," Kandar said. In the darkness, Ben could only just see the outline of the muscle of his shoulders shifting as he moved closer. "Did anyone check for a fairy glamour on the body? Or on the envoy, before he disappeared?"

"A fairy glamour?" Ben said blankly. "Why would fairies have anything to do with it?"

"Or he could have been a fairy himself," Kandar said. "Do you know what happened to the body after? Was anyone watching that it didn't turn to leaves and ash?" He leaned even closer. The night before, when he had followed Ben to his chamber, he had been so close that the beer on his breath had mixed with the overpowering smell of goblin. It was not a bad smell, earthy, overlaid with hay and horse and a strange note from very far away. This morning his breath smelled like herbal tea, spicy with sea bay.

He was not listening to what Kandar was saying, only letting the rhythm of syllables move over him.

But he had spoken a familiar name, and its ugliness twisted Ben out of his reverie.

"Taryn," he repeated. A familiar storm of emotions rose in his chest—betrayal, fury, and bewilderment. "You still haven't told me what happened to Taryn. You must know. She would not—she would not have let go the crown of her own free will."

"She did not," Kandar said. He hesitated, then said, "Has truly no news come to you on the goblin road?"

"Nothing has come up the road in the seven years between you and me," Ben said. The goblin's sudden reticence tasted strange in the intimacy before the stove. "You don't need to spare my feelings. We were friends once, but—I saw what she was becoming, and—what direction she meant to go on. I am not surprised she came to disaster. You will not shock me."

"I think I will," the goblin said, his voice grim. "You have not spoken with Taryn in eleven years."

"I left seven years ago," Ben corrected.

"I know. Taryn left three years before that."

"But—but she—"

"The queen you took for Taryn was the daughter of Oberon, treacherous king of fairies," the goblin said. "Taryn, daughter of Ardloch, sister of Elsyn, was stolen away, and stolen again by my cousin, the king of goblins, and is now his queen in the mountains."

His words washed over Ben like chunks of ice hurled down a mountain waterfall. "But then—she—what proof—*Elsyn*—"

"Think," Kandar said forcefully. "*Think*. You knew, didn't you? You knew that it wasn't her."

Ben thought. The change had been so sudden and so brutal. He could remember the expression on Elsyn's face and the sound of Taryn's laughter, though not the words or even the court hanger-on who had said them. He remembered doors that had always been open to him suddenly closed in his face. He remembered the rumors that had started to circulate, about things he had never been ashamed of before they were mocked. He remembered his mother's exhaustion.

He had thought he would cook in his own anger. Taryn had always had a biting tongue and a quick wit from earliest childhood, and she had often said true things that cut. But she had been quick to apologize and rigid in her own dignity. Overnight she had gathered a flock of toadies, whose inane observations she chortled at and whose petty rivalries she stoked to rampant cruelty. Her behavior had disgusted him, nearly as much as Elsyn's avoidance had injured him.

But if the horrible creature who had done all of that had *not been Taryn*—

"I have to go back," he whispered. "I have to go back *right now*."

The priests were making cheese in the ducal kitchen.

As Elsyn watched, two of them, both wearing long shifts of

undyed linen, used metal spatulas to scoop bricks of drained curd from a great metal vat suspended over the hearth. A low fire burned beneath. The curd-bricks were laid out end to end on the great table running the length of the room. A third priest, holding a worryingly large knife, stepped forward and diced furiously, moving from one end of the table to the other in a smooth progression. One of the other priests, a young person with a shaven head, walked behind her, sprinkling salt from a large bag over the chopped curd.

"Where's the milk coming from?" Elsyn asked. She stood just behind Algenymmar of Deragcaish, highest-ranking of all nobles who had survived the false Taryn's brief and horrible rule, mother of Elsyn's one-time friend, in the door of the kitchen. Elsyn noted with some surprise that they were now the same height, fully a head taller than anyone else in the kitchen, and roughly the same width. Algenymmar had always seemed enormous when she was a child, a giant who could pick up her horse and carry it back to the stable if it threw a shoe.

The priests had glanced up when the duke appeared in the doorway, but they were apparently accustomed enough to her presence to do no more than bow and continue on with cheesemaking. Algenymmar seemed disinclined to interrupt them.

The duke looked tired and angry up close, but the deep lines around her mouth relaxed somewhat as she watched the curd being worked.

Her shoulders jerked in an odd motion. "I don't know," she said brusquely, then, seeming to think better of her tone, "I did not set them to this task. The first priests who sheltered in my house took over this kitchen for their own cheeses—their own uses. Other priests bring them the milk, and take away the cheese. It's like they can't stop themselves." Elsyn wasn't sure if that last muttered comment was meant for her.

She had never been in this kitchen before. In the palace, she and Taryn had known enough back hallways and interpersonal dynamics among the serving staff to squirrel Ben away to little-traversed attics, courtyards, and storage closets. They had weaseled themselves through any numbers of kitchens and stolen alarming quantities of fruit and pastries. Their parents had neither time nor interest enough to limit such explorations.

When they had been guests in the ducal house, their activities had been restrained to things that could be done while sitting stiffly upright on one of the uncomfortable divans in the parlor. Elsyn had always been scared of Algenymmar.

She was still scared of Algenymmar.

Now the chopping priest had brought out a mold, a huge cylindrical thing carved of dark wood. Elsyn bit back an exclamation. The great aged cheeses made by palace priests had once generated a large amount of money and acclaim for the temple. A pattern cut into the side of the mold—two profiles facing one another inside a horned oval—marked it as one of the palace's own special cheeses. The priests set the mold on two wooden blocks inside a basin to catch the draining whey, then laid a cloth inside and began to pack it with curd.

No great cheeses had been made in the palace temple for years now. There hadn't been the spare milk, the priests to make it, or the markets to sell them. What did it mean that these priests had the milk to do one now? They must still have access to herds, herds close by, which somehow hadn't been reported to the palace. Where had they gotten the cheese mold? Were there still priests sneaking back into the palace regularly? She didn't recognize these three, so they must have come from somewhere out in the country. But they were being sheltered by the Duke, who clearly had some arrangement with Neddie or the High Priest. So—

"How long," she said finally, through the buzz of questions in her skull, "have you been hosting my temple siblings?"

Now the mold had been filled to bursting. The lid was set into the top of the mold and weighted, and the priests shared among themselves a piece of the cheese which had not gone into the press. Once again, the image of Kandar taking a piece of curd from her hand with his teeth suddenly, vividly unfolded in her head, and Elsyn's face grew warm.

Algenymmar responded as though she had not spoken. "Can you control your—your *cow?*"

Elsyn cast a glance behind her, where Bean had laid down in the corridor and was now chewing her cud luxuriously. The goblins had agreed to wait upstairs, but she had insisted one of the cows accompany her. Bean had angled herself so that her rump and massive horns blocked the hall. Two people wearing ducal livery and worried expressions stood behind her. Turnip had vanished. Hopefully she had embarked on a fact-finding mission and was not currently employed in plundering the kitchen garden.

Bean closed one eye very slowly. LADY SMELLS FAMILIAR, she commented.

Elsyn wished she knew what to make of that. "She is a holy beast of the Two-Bodied God, and lead cow of the temple herd," she said. "I can make polite suggestions, but I may not make demands."

To give her credit, Algenymmar did not suggest that a queen ought to have more authority over her animals. Properly speaking, Bean did not belong to anyone, not even the God. "Please suggest that she wait in the courtyard."

"She has serious concerns about my safety," Elsyn said. The familiar, delicious smell of the cheese and the presence of the tremendous cow a few feet away made her suddenly reckless. Ben's mother was clearly allied with the temple, even if she was no friend to the royal house. "I was recently attacked by an unknown party, by surprise, under cover of darkness. If one of the holy cattle had not been with me, I might have suffered great injury."

She paused, holding her breath, wondering if she had pushed too far and too fast.

The expression of the older woman did not change, but a muscle under her eye twitched. "A grave concern indeed," she agreed. "Who do you believe was responsible?"

Elsyn took a deep breath. She suddenly wished she had thought this tactic through a bit more. She didn't know if Algenymmar was responsible for the attack on her, but the duke was fully capable of murdering any number of people. "I am not yet sure," she said, fighting to keep her voice even. "I am sure you are aware of the difficulties my sister left behind her." Was that polite enough? She hoped it was polite enough. "I had hoped you might have some insight."

"As you have said, there are many forces at work in the kingdom, Your Majesty," the duke said, her voice as rigid as granite.

This isn't going anywhere! Elsyn thought desperately. She's been out in the world playing conversational chess with scheming nobles while I've been stuffed away talking to cows for ten years. What could I possibly say that would make her listen?

The duke's voice cut through her thoughts like a knife. "Why did you send for my son?"

"What?"

The duke turned slightly so she faced the younger woman directly. Behind her shoulder, the priests paused in their cleaning and looked up. "Why did you send for my son, *Elsyn?*" Her voice had dropped so low it was barely audible, and it shook with anger. "His name has not been spoken in many years, by you or anyone else."

Elsyn met her gaze squarely. Her guts felt like knots made of knots.

The truth, of course, would never do—that she had said Ben's name in a flash of desperation and sadness; that she had not thought what impact her words might have beyond ending the horrible marriage-meeting with the horrible men sizing her up like a mountain to be climbed. So far as she knew, Kandar was the only one who had left to go searching. She hadn't wanted to think about it, but she supposed he would return empty-handed at some point, perhaps with a story about the death of the man he sought. She would have to figure out what to do at that point, but she didn't know yet.

If Ben had wanted to come back, he would have come back. She didn't know why he had left without a word of explanation, but clearly the need to be gone had outweighed everything else.

"He was my friend, a good and true one," she heard her own voice say. "I find myself in great need of friends now."

Algenymmar's eyes changed almost imperceptibly. "I wonder if he is a good a man as you remember."

PART THREE

Telwulf was not happy to let Ben go. She followed him through the goblin village while he made his preparations to leave, trailed by smaller goblins in various states of distress. Her arguments began very reasonably and quickly degraded to cajoling and threats, echoed by her retinue.

"—you'd be taking a stupid risk. You've told me about how poisonous that queen of theirs is, and you want to wade back in among the goat shit—"

"—*goat shit*—"

"—why risk it? They don't deserve you, and who will take your place in the eeling boat? You've a fine hand with the eel spear, nearly as good as Telgol—"

"—*eel* spear—"

"—and in any case Quince is *retired,* you can't take a horse out of retirement, think what it'll do to his digestion—"

"—to his *digestion*—"

Ben and Kandar had finally departed three days later, their saddlebags stuffed with goat cheese and dried fish. Telwulf embraced Ben fiercely and glared at Kandar. "Come back if you can," she said, her voice stern.

"I don't know—" Ben started, a hollow feeling in his chest.

"Come back *if you can,*" Telwulf almost shouted, and her eyes glistened. "Now go! Do what you must do!"

They rode away down the goblin road, away from the goats grazing on the bluffs looking out over the goblin sea, and back into the human kingdom.

The grass unfolded before them in unforgiving waves of yellow and brown. Ben reined up Quince and surveyed the plain grimly. "How long did it take you to ride here?" he asked.

Socks pranced and bucked, kicking his hind legs, but Kandar held onto the saddle with hands and feet like this was perfectly normal. Quince laid his ears back and snorted.

"About a week," Kandar yelled over his shoulder.

"But—" Socks was already away, galloping, sometimes jumping. There was no way Kandar could hear Ben's voice telling him that it had taken him three months to cross the plains on horseback.

Ben tapped his heel against Quince's side, and the gelding heaved himself into a walk, then leaned into a canter. The wind took hold of his hair and pulled tears from his eyes, and Ben suddenly laughed. He had rarely ridden during his time among the goblins, who got around on foot and by boat and occasionally by goat-cart. He hadn't realized he'd missed this. Quince pointed his nose at the flash of white in Socks' tail, and they followed.

The feeling of the horse's hooves steadily eating up the distance, the wind, and the hard blue of the sky held him tightly, suspended between the sun and the earth. The harsh light, undimmed by a single cloud, struck the grass like a hammer striking a bell.

When Kandar pulled Socks back and fell into a trot beside him, Ben jerked as though he had fallen from a great height. He turned in the saddle, bracing for another round of questions about Elsyn.

"Did the sea-goblins tell you anything of their history?" Kandar asked.

Ben blinked, caught off-guard. Socks noticed a clump of new grass and skidded to a halt to sniff at it; Quince slowed to a walk again. The sun had moved low in the sky, and the contours of the landscape had changed dramatically, sweeping down to a river in the distance. Kandar jumped down from Socks' back and dug in his saddlebags.

"If we're taking a rest, I can cook something," Ben said, still thinking. What had Telwulf told him about how the goblins had come to the sea?

Kandar kicked at the clump of green grass—still more yellow than anything in the pocket-world behind them. "There's water here. A spring. You can see the mud on the other side."

He went to work digging out around the spring, while Ben dismounted and rummaged in his own packs.

"You can take his tack off," Kandar said. "We've made good time. Quince got hold of Socks' tailwind and kept up far better than I expected." He huffed approvingly at the gelding, who lipped the sleeve of his coat.

Ben looked around them again, wondering how much more

ground they had covered in the last few hours than a normal pair of riders, as magic had made a straight path through the grass and tumbled rocks from their way.

There were wild onions growing around the spring and a savory-smelling bush he recognized as a kind of sage. The smell provoked a memory of Telwulf and Telgol smoking together, telling a story in turns, sometimes singing. "The goblins came to the sea from far away," he said, lifting onions bulbs and cutting silvery leaves with his knife. "In the time of Telshind's great-great-great-grandmother, and she's one of the oldest in the tribe now."

"What are those for?" Kandar asked, leaning over his shoulder.

"Soup," Ben said mildly. "Unless you'd like to eat plain dried fish." Kandar wrinkled his nose.

"They had been forced to leave," Ben said, wracking his brain for the rest of the memory. He cut grass and knotted it, making a pile for their cooking fire. "There had been a dispute between two different families over territorial rights."

The goblin saw what he was doing and drew his sword, using it to scythe the grass from around their camp. "In the mountains? Where in the mountains? It wouldn't be a fight over the castle," he went on, without pausing for Ben to answer, "But there's a ring of stones back up on the ridge, I always thought that might have been a tower, long ago. . ." He wiped his sword and sheathed it, looking at Ben expectantly.

"I don't remember anything about mountains," Ben said, steadily knotting tinder. "Telgol said her grandmother had told her that they sailed their boats down a great river to the sea. They found the wild goats there when they arrived, and the caves, and small yellow flowers blooming on all the bushes. They had to learn new ways to make boats, because hardly any trees grow by the sea, and the ones there are small and crumpled."

Kandar gathered a heavy armful of cut grass and carried it to where Ben was working. He squatted down next to him, companionably bumping knees, and tied more grass knots. He glanced up at Kandar, orange eyes luminous. "What river is that? There's no river that goes through the goblin kingdom that you could take a boat down. All of them have waterfalls and long stretches of stony water."

"I'm only telling you what was told me," Ben said, sparking his flint off his knife, sending sparks into a pile of grass knots stacked in a depression carved into the dirt. They lit with gratifying quickness. It was a terrible relief to talk about something other than Elsyn or his mother. "Isn't it possible that your people didn't always live in the mountains?

Maybe your ancestors and my—the sea goblins started out somewhere else and went in opposite directions."

"Possible?" Kandar repeated. He paced around the fire on all fours. Socks flipped his mane and tried to bite Kandar's crest, but the goblin stopped him with a hand. Quince huffed a sigh and moved to another patch of grass. "Maybe it is. I don't know. The goblins—my family—before the horse-lords came, they'd all gone to stone."

"Stone?" Ben looked up from the fire. "What do you mean?"

"I always thought it was just a thing that happened to goblins," Kandar said. "A sort of normal thing, if we sit still too long. If we wait for too long. But turning to stone does something funny to your head. My father didn't remember much, past when he woke up. Even if I'd known to ask him where his father had come from, I don't think he could have told me."

"And the horse-lords woke them," Ben said. "Who were they? Where did they come from?"

"My mother's people," Kandar said. "They were humans, more or less—it's hard to say, because they came into the mountains so long ago. My mother and her sisters smelled like humans, but they used magic like goblins."

"Humans can use magic," Ben said, chopping his greens against a smooth stone.

"Not in the same way," Kandar said. "Can I have an onion?"

Ben passed him one, and Kandar popped the whole bulb into his mouth. "Can you get clean water from the spring, do you think?" Ben asked.

Perhaps that was one of the goblin magics, he thought, because Kandar returned a few minutes later with a full flask of sweet water. He settled down on his haunches to watch Ben cook. "Ildar is one of the horse-lords," he said, his eyes tracking Ben's hands. "The king's wizard. He was born just before they rode up into the mountains and set their tents upon the king's court, and he's aged like a goblin."

"Not at all?" Ben guessed. He took a canvas-wrapped lump from the pack and cracked it against the rock, breaking the hard fish inside to pieces.

"Not in ways you'd recognize," Kandar said, sounding thoughtful. "I think he remembers, sometimes, that the humans have gone on without him, and it grieves him."

Ben thought of all the ways the kingdom of his birth could have changed in seven years, and he flinched. "Is your father—" He bit off the question and busied himself with the soup-pan.

Kandar's tail lashed. "Gone stony again," he said briefly. "He hasn't spoken for a long time."

Ben wondered how many years a *long time* was.

"What about your father?" Kandar asked. "Did he agree to let you be banished?"

The fish became translucent and then disintegrated into shreds when it hit the warming water. Ben focused intently on the blurring edges of a piece bobbing about in the boiling soup. "I'm not sure what my father would have done," he said, stirring the soup with the tip of his knife. "He died when I was very young." The sky blued around them, and in the isolated familiarity of a camp wreathed in soup-steam, he went on, "I am more like him than I am like my mother, I have been told. He was the third son of a minor family, and I do not think he spent every moment of his childhood thinking about the honor of their house." He stopped. There were other things he could say—other true things—about his mother and the line of Deragcaish, but once he said them, even into the silent, grass-perfumed air, they would exist as truths, and not just shadowy suppositions.

"I would have liked to meet him," Kandar said.

Ben dug out spoons and bowls from his pack. The soup was a little thin, but the salt from the fish and the onion at least gave it a strong warm flavor. "This isn't half-bad. What do you mean?"

"I think he was probably a good man," said Kandar, dipping his bowl in the pot.

"How would you sneak a cheese mold out of the temple?" Elsyn asked, staring at the priest-door.

"Is that a question for me?" Jolar asked, scratching her chin.

"Could one of the priests have left it on a cheese when they sold it?" Amlar asked. "Or given it to one of the palace servants to take into the city."

Elsyn considered this as the three of them sized up the rusted gate in the palace wall, wide enough to admit a one-horse cart. A cobblestone road led down to the gate from a courtyard at the side of the temple, but between the knee-high grass and the loose stones, it was in terrible repair. She had not come down this way in years. "I had thought

71

all of the palace staff were too scared of my—of the false queen to risk such a thing, but the High Priest has been disguising themself as a servant for months."

"Hard to say what they might have managed with the Duke helping them on the outside," said Amlar, sounding thoughtful. Her large triangular ears flipped back as she considered.

That was indeed the sticking point, and the main reason Elsyn wanted the priest-door operational again as soon as possible. The more she thought about the milk needed to make the great cheeses—the practiced way the three priests had moved through the chopping and salting of curd, as though they had done it a hundred times in that very kitchen—and, for that matter, the fact that the High Priest hadn't been discovered in the two years after their assumed death—the more certain she was that some large part of the temple network had survived. Algenymmar, whatever she had said about not knowing where the milk came from, had to be involved. Perhaps the cows were on one of the ducal properties.

She desperately needed to find out what was left, and she wanted as few people as possible to know what she knew.

Two stumpy towers stood on either side of the priest-door, bulging past the contour of the massive walls of the palace enclosure. Elsyn's mouth went dry when she looked at them. When she was a child, this gate had been staffed by a dozen priests, checking shipments of grain and hay, taking cheese orders from merchants, and directing petitioners and those seeking veterinary care to the various parts of the temple. A single soldier, armed with a baton, had stood in the background to discourage any exasperated farmers from getting too rude. It had been exciting to hide in the grass with Ben and Taryn and watch the various people and animals do their business.

When the false Taryn had been crowned, those priests had been replaced by two soldiers carrying long-knives and crossbows. Once they had become jailers, the soldiers no longer looked to the residents of the temple with deference. The High Priest had told the initiates to stay sixty paces from the gate at all times.

"There's no one there," Amlar said, breaking into her reverie. "There haven't been soldiers at this gate for three weeks."

"The palace guard runs itself without you?" Jolar asked, a heavy note of disapproval in her voice.

"Obviously," Elsyn said, too shaken by the towers to be rude. "Amlar, is the door itself still secure? Have there been people going in and out this way?"

They walked closer. Two heavy oaken bars slotted into the stone at the sides of the gate, lifted by winches operated from inside the towers. Elsyn's shoulders felt like granite.

"There's a door into the tower on this side," Amlar said. "Based on the rust, the gate hasn't been opened much in recent days."

Elsyn glanced behind her, where the herd had formed a knot next to the priest-road. The grass was not good there, but she could feel Bean watching her. She made a small gesture that the veterinary priests usually made over a sewn-up wound—Two-bodied God, it is out of my hands—before following Jolar over the threshold.

The door opened into a tight spiral staircase that wound upward to a single round room, lit by an arrowslit facing the exterior and a small glazed window facing the interior. Amlar had understated the rust; it encrusted the crank that raised the bars on the gate.

Elsyn sneezed. A heavy drift of dust had built up between the wall and the crank. "I can't remember the last time I saw it open."

She felt, rather than saw, the goblins exchange looks. "Eight weeks," Jolar said.

"What?"

"This is the way the king came and went from the palace. Our king, when he and your sister and the witch killed the impostor. The guard opened it for them. Ildar told us."

The last soldiers here had left wadded-up bits of miscellaneous trash stuck in a gap in the mortar near the floor. Elsyn kicked at it, waiting for her heartbeat to slow. The phrase *your sister* hung in the air. She tipped her head head back and looked at the rafters. There was more trash stuck up there. What had the guards been doing in their free time?

In the silence, Amlar swiped dust off the mechanism and tested the crank. A horrible, creaking screech filled the room, and she stopped.

Finally Elsyn's mouth could form words, but they were not the words she intended to say. "How close is Kandar to the king?"

"They are foster siblings," Jolar said. "They can be no closer."

"So," Elsyn said slowly, "if the king had told him to marry me for —for stability in the kingdom, or as some sort of defense against the fairies—he would have done it."

Amlar and Jolar passed another look between them.

"He would have if he had been asked, that is true," Amlar said, leaning heavily on the crank handle. It screamed again, and all three of them jumped.

"None of us knew that this was Kandar's intention. I don't think Kandar knew that this was his intention, until he saw you. He told the king he meant to be back in the mountains within the month. It is," and here Jolar's voice took on a note somewhere between affection and exasperation, "not unlike Kandar to fall so violently in love."

Elsyn's mind froze, but her face grew hot. "Then he'll soon think better of it," she forced out.

"He won't," said Jolar and Amlar at once.

"You must be joking," Elsyn said, and it sounded feeble even in her own ears. "I can't—that's not—of course that's not possible. Do you think you can get the door mechanism to work? Is it broken? I don't think it's broken—"

"It needs oiling, and the nails in the gate hinges will need replacing, if there are going to be people using it daily," Amlar replied promptly. "Yes, I can."

"Good, then we'll do that," Elsyn said, turning to flee down the stairs. She couldn't fathom what reason the goblins would have for lying to her, and it was such a strange lie to tell—of *course* Kandar hadn't offered for her because he wanted *her*, there was some sort of practical reason— the power he'd gain as consort, or—perhaps he thought she'd make him cheese every day—

She didn't realize she had gone down more stairs than she'd come up until a flickering of light across the stones caught her eye. She stopped and blinked. Daylight streamed down the stairs behind her, but a different light, a warm glow like lantern-light, cast a thin shadow across the curved surface in front of her.

Elsyn turned and looked up; a doorway gaped at the top of the steps. The entrance to the tower stood open on the other side. Jolar's crest and ears and then her eyes appeared around the edge of the frame.

"This wasn't here before," she said.

"Who's there?" called out a voice from below.

It was such a familiar voice that Elsyn, not thinking about enemies or attacks or political machinations, called back, "It's Elsyn. I'm coming down."

"*Elsyn!*" the voice said, as she reached the bottom step. Jolar's claws scratched on the stone behind her.

The basement room was no larger than the guard room above, but where that chamber had been empty and dusty, this one was packed with shelves, laden with round, cylindrical packages. *Cheeses.* A short, plump woman stood in the pool of lantern-light, an open crate at her feet.

"Petra," Elsyn said, her mouth producing the name without her mind's input. Her ears registered what she had said, and her throat tightened. Petra had had the bunk above Elsyn for the first four years of initiate priesthood. She had been loud and affectionate toward everyone, including the cows and the despised younger sister of the queen.

Elsyn had always assumed that this was why Petra had disappeared with no warning.

"Thank the God in Their Bodies, you can help me with this," Petra said, as though it had been a week and not years. What had once been a dusting of freckles over her pale skin had turned into a dense stippling, almost like a tan, and when she squatted down next to the crate Elsyn saw that her curly brown hair had been bleached pale. "We've just set up down here—blessed nuisance it was to carry the cheeses through the other tower and down this one, but the High Priest said not to mess about with the gate—"

The crate, when she stepped closer, held neat stacks of small bark-wrapped cheeses.

"I can't stand doing the wrappings," Petra went on. "But they're dead easy to slip in someone's window at night, and they stay good for weeks." She looked over Elsyn's shoulder. "Who's that?"

"Her dignity, the honorable Jolar," Elsyn said. She really had to learn the goblins' proper titles.

"And this is?" Jolar said, a hint of threat in her voice.

"This is my friend Petra," Elsyn said. The word *friend* fell from her mouth easily, and she shot a glance at the other woman, thinking surely she would correct the assumption, because Elsyn did not have friends, the false Taryn had made sure of that—

"Yes, old friends," Petra said. "I taught you how to feel the hind leg to see if the cow's about to kick your bucket over, do you remember that?"

Jolar came down the steps, her face relaxing into its regular half-smirk, and was now inspecting the shelves. Petra looked at her and then at Elsyn, raising her eyebrows high.

"Soon to be your in-law?" she stage-whispered.

"I," Elsyn said. "Well."

"Yes," Jolar said.

"Fill this up with cheeses," Petra said, passing Elsyn an odd garment, a skirt covered in a grid of pockets. "One per pouch."

Elsyn considered the skirt. "You've been distributing food in secret?"

"Hasn't the High Priest spoken with you about it?" Petra asked, looking up. A divot sat between her eyebrows. "I thought now that the monst—forgive me—the queen was dead—"

Jolar snorted. Elsyn spread the skirt across an empty shelf and pushed cheese after cheese into its voluminous storage. "You know where to find the High Priest?"

"Of course," Petra said. "They've been in hiding in the duke's house since Taryn tried to kill them."

Chalk up another reason she had to speak to Algenymmar again, Elsyn thought grimly.

"Is it safe to warehouse the cheese here?" she asked, not wanting to lose her temper over the behavior of the High Priest. "Anyone might come in that door. As I am constantly being reminded," she glanced at Jolar, "I do not have control over who comes and goes through the palace right now."

"How do you mean?" Petra asked, sounding puzzled. "Here, and now this—herbal packets. I've two families with the summer rash, and three with the river runs. There." She pointed at a half-dozen baskets on the top shelf, each stuffed with dried plants.

"Can I help?" Jolar asked.

"Might as well. Most of the good in the herbs came from the magic-workers who did charms with them. Now it's mostly to comfort the parents." She went back to rummaging on the bottom shelf. "The only people who know the sign to open the door are priests."

Elsyn, her hands full of dried oregano and feverfew, took a moment to parse that last sentence, and then another to work out what Petra was talking about. *Two-bodied God, it is out of my hands.* The wound-healing gesture must have been set as the key to whatever spell closed the doorway.

She noticed that Jolar was muttering under her breath as she stuffed herbs into cloth packets. Please, Elsyn thought, let goblin magic work on sick humans.

"The High Priest has not been entirely forthcoming with me," she said.

Petra looked up at her.

Elsyn remembered a night soon after she had been initiated into the temple. A farmer had carried a heavily-pregnant goat through the gate. The animal had been struggling to give birth for hours. One of the veterinary priests—had it been Rononya? Elsyn thought it had been Rononya—had pulled a dead kid, and then two more tiny, premature babies. The mother had hemorrhaged suddenly and died, and the surviving kids had been given to the initiates to bottle-feed. Petra had demanded that she be allowed to take charge of one kid, and Elsyn the other. They had sat up in the cold hours of the morning, each with a goat kid wrapped in their robe, poking cloth teats attached to jars of milk under the noses of their charges every few hours. Elsyn had been too frightened of her goat dying to talk much, but Petra sang in a low voice and told stories about her family's farm in the far west, where the cattle were as furry as sheep.

"They haven't told me anything," Elsyn said. "I am making out as best I can with the cows and the goblin emissaries." She nodded to Jolar, who nodded back.

Petra was quiet for a minute as she nailed the crate up and shoved it back onto a shelf. Elsyn wondered if she remembered the night with the goat kids as clearly.

"I thought there was something amiss," she said finally. "The duke has been acting something strange since that—since the queen died." A doubtful note had entered Petra's voice, and she looked at Elsyn as though she had suddenly become a stranger.

Elsyn took a deep breath, fighting the desire to clench her fists in her shift. "I need your help," she said, and her voice shook only a little. She felt the eyes of Petra and Jolar on her, and they burned. The High Priest clearly doesn't trust me, she thought. And I need to convince Petra that she still can. "I was not trained how to be queen. I do not know how to talk to nobles—" I only know how to run from their children when they're bullying me, she thought, and even that I'm a little rusty on "—or have careful conversations or play games where everyone talks about one thing and pretends it's something else. I know how to take care of cows and how to make cheese." She caught her breath. "But maybe—maybe it isn't such a far way from knowing do those things and taking care of people. I think I can be a sort of queen who takes care of people. I need help from those who know how to do that, who have *been* doing that, all this time."

Elsyn could not look Petra in the eye after this little speech, so she stared at her eyebrows. "Do you think you can put me in contact with some of the priests who have kept up the communications between temples?"

Petra took the strange skirt full of cheeses off the shelf, fastened it about her midsection, then shouldered her way into another robe. Her face kept moving, folding into expression after expression, as she thought.

Finally she stood in front of Elsyn, looking like an overstuffed dumpling, her face resolved into lines of determination. "Let me pass these out," she said. "I'll be back here just after dark, and then we will talk."

Quince's steady trot had lulled Ben into a doze when Socks screamed and fell.

His gelding, who had not spooked at leaping goats, goblin children trying to climb on his back, or boat sails snapping in the wind, reared and pawed at the air. Ben yelled and only just kept his seat, grabbing the saddle with both hands. The horse whinnied in panic, and he pressed himself against Quince's neck, chanting nonsense phrases—"A good horse, a fine horse, nothing ruffles your feathers, you've the smoothest feathers of any horse I've ever met. . ." After a minute that felt like hours, Quince dropped to all fours. The grass, magically open to their passage a minute ago, rose to Quince's neck and pressed against them on all sides. Socks' flailing was visible only as a violent shaking of the seed heads.

Kandar was shouting, but Ben was too dazed to understand what he was saying. The sensation of suddenly crashing to earth after skimming along just above the surface dizzied him. Whatever magic let them travel so quickly must be tied to Socks, and now that Socks had fallen—

Panic seized him, and he swung down from Quince's saddle, stumbled, and rushed forward again. What could they do if Socks had broken a leg? *How* could he have broken a leg, running just above the land as he did?

He plowed forward, shoving through dense stands of grass. The blades and stems caught and cut at his hands, his face, his clothes. "Kandar! Kandar, what's happened?"

Kandar let out a long, ululating howl of rage. Ben's skin crawled.

One of Socks' back hooves flashed across the ground, almost smashing his ankle, and he skipped back and to the left. The horse was down on the ground, sprawled on his side, flailing all his limbs so hard that if he hadn't broken anything yet he soon would. The horse slammed his neck against the ground with terrifying force, but it was not enough to free himself. Strands of grass wrapped his chest, his forelegs, and his neck, so dense that they hid shiny black of his hide. Ben got a glimpse of terrified, white-rimmed eye, and then heard a familiar mind-voice, distorted by terror.

Help! Oh, help! They're pulling me down!

Socks' front hooves up to his hocks had disappeared into a hole in the ground. It looked no bigger than the entrance to a badger sett, but the ground rippled around it, like a snake distending itself to swallow a larger prey. Ben circled the horse, drawing his knife, until he was out of reach of the striking hooves, then sliced at the creeping, snaking stuff winding around Socks' back. Where the steel blade hit the grass, it blackened and shriveled, emitting a foul smell.

"Gods help us," Ben whispered. Praying he didn't hit the horse, he cut upward, slashing at the plants strangling him. One slash—two—that had been too deep—a line of blood oozed up from the horse's skin—three—suddenly Socks had his head free, and his mouth darted forward to snap at the grass wrapped around his forelegs.

"Don't kick me in the head," Ben said, as though Socks was in any state to listen to him, and stabbed savagely into the hole from where the grass grew. The blade hit something—please let that not be a hoof, he repeated fervently to himself, please, *please*—and then something else. If only goblins shoed their horses, Socks could have defended himself against whatever this was—

Abruptly the grass wrapping Socks' body went slack and ashy, crumbling as the horse lurched to his feet.

The thing Socks said was not words but a distraught image, of waves of grass shaping themselves into dozens of hands, seizing Kandar's tail and leg, pulling him to the ground.

Ben spun around—surely Kandar couldn't have been taken far, it had only been a few minutes—and saw Quince's head rise over the grass just to his left, his ears tight against his head and his top lip skinned back. Ben shoved around a particularly massive clump of grass—he had forgotten how much he hated traveling through wild country—and saw a bizarre sight: a grass-wrapped lump, horribly like a shrouded corpse, slowly being dragged toward him. He looked down and realized that he stood behind another pulsing hole in the earth, this one larger and darker, with ropes of malevolent grass stretching from its maw over the ground. The magical badger sett apparently had more than one entrance. Quince stood just outside the reach of the snaking grass, panting, half-rearing, and stamping the ground, his nostrils red and his eyes white with terror. He didn't want to leave Ben, but he was so frightened that sweat darkened his neck.

Something else caught Ben's eye, a silver glimmer in the grass. Kandar's sword had been torn from his belt and thrown across the earth, leaving a blackened trail of wilted vegetation where it had touched.

Steel, Ben thought, whatever it is can't bear the touch of steel, and rather than set his feet down on the writhing, gripping grass, he jumped, landing hard in another stand of grass, this one filled with sharp edges. He rolled over and scrabbled for the hilt of the weapon.

Something like a hand closed around his ankle. Yelling, he brought the blade up and down, severing the grass tentacle.

At the same moment, a dark arm thrust free of the grass mummy being dragged toward the hole. A short knife was clutched in Kandar's clawed fist.

"Kandar!" Ben bellowed. "*Your sword!*" He turned the hilt away from himself and tossed the weapon, cursing himself for a fool as soon as it left his hand—

Kandar caught the hilt and swung his blade in a wide arc, severing the grass that held him fast. A horrible scream echoed from inside the magical badger sett. Kandar rolled to his feet and leaped toward it, but the dark holes on either side of the enormous clump of grass abruptly collapsed in on themselves, with a slithering sound like a dead squid falling from a net. Just as suddenly, the grass around them shivered and settled again into place, becoming less tall, less dense, and less saturated with queasy color and movement.

Kandar screamed in rage again, throwing down his sword and digging at the earth mound with both hands. Dirt clods flew to either side of him, but they appeared to be wholly unmagical dirt clods.

Ben slowly got to his feet, heart hammering in his ears. "Socks?" he gasped. "Did he break anything? Is he all right?"

Kandar stopped digging immediately and jerked to his feet. "Socks!" he yelled. "Socks! Where are you? I have to look at your feet! *I have a snack for you!*"

Socks poked his head through the grass. Yes, I would like a snack, I am a very mighty warrior, he said. I would have *not* have let the fairies ride me if they pulled me down into the hill. I am very fierce.

Kandar slid his hands up and down the horse's legs to check each joint for bruising, though Socks was so worked up that he kept pulling away to stamp his feet and toss his head.

I am *very* fierce, he insisted. I was only *surprised.* I am very fierce!

Ben tugged an old shirt free from one of his saddlebags and vigorously rubbed Quince's withers, back, and hindquarters. After a few minutes, the gelding rested his head on Ben's shoulder.

"You are a magnificent horse," he whispered. "If you hadn't stopped when you did, we'd all have been caught."

Quince thought that was likely true. He wanted to be away from this evil spot.

"No broken bones," Kandar called. "He's got a cut on his neck —"

Guilt washed over Ben. "That's me—I was trying to get him loose —"

"You *did* get him loose," Kandar said.

"Quince wants to leave now," Ben said, embarrassed, hoisting himself into the saddle. He waited until Kandar had shaken himself thoroughly and pulled himself onto Socks' back before clucking his tongue at the gelding. They set off at a walk, Socks periodically dancing sideways with nerves. "Kandar, what *was* that?"

"Fairies," the goblin said, shooting a look behind them. "A door into a fairy hill opened, and they tried to pull Socks in."

Ben thought of the grass forming itself into dozens of grasping little hands and shuddered. "I've never heard of that happening before."

"It probably didn't, before a fairy queen sat on the human throne for seven years," Kandar said, his voice grim.

"Are you all right?" Ben asked.

"Are you?" Kandar said.

They looked at each other for a long minute. Ben's stomach did a slow flip.

The secret cheese warehouse in the lower city was more like a secret cheese closet. This space was half as big as the tower basement, with a natural outcropping of bedrock slanting one wall and making it useless for storage.

Petra pointed at one shelf. "These are more of the cheeses to give out; they're fast to make and easy to hide in a pocket." She pointed at another. "These are the cheeses we've aged. There are still merchants who will pay a pretty sum for genuine temple cheese."

"This is a lot of cheese," Emar, Jolar's nephew said, sounding bewildered. Elsyn privately wished that Jolar could have accompanied her, but she had politely declared herself unavailable for tonight. Emar was very young and very delicate of limb, with long, graceful hands and a stance like a dancer's, and standing next to him made Elsyn feel like an animate wardrobe.

Three priests were in the corner of the cellar, methodically cutting tiny testing cores from the oldest and largest wheels. Elsyn recognized one of them from the ducal kitchen, but the other two were unfamiliar to her.

"This is Hinat," Petra said, nodding to a burly person with a shaved head and bushy brows, their skin burnt a deep brown color. They had biceps as big around as melons. "They came back to the city with me."

Petra had not spoken much about what had happened to her after she had disappeared from the palace temple. The temple where she had ended up was in the south of the country, far enough distant that they had sometimes hosted sailors who had come over the great sea and through the independent baronies.

"Stop eating that!" Hinat barked. Elsyn jumped, before she realized they weren't talking to her. Turning, she watched Emar pop two barked-wrapped cheeses into his mouth, one in each cheek. He had taken them from a crate shoved into the corner, at a distance from the other shelves. Woven grass medallions hung from each corner of the box. Looking at them make Elsyn's eyes water.

Petra hissed between her teeth. "Spit those out right now," she said, her voice suddenly authoritative. "Those cheeses are contaminated."

"What do you—" Elsyn started to ask, but suddenly Emar gagged and pawed at his throat. She thought for a moment that he had just swallowed too quickly. Then he spat with sudden force, pushing one of the small cheeses out of his mouth, where it hung in the air, suspended by white, furry strands—strands which writhed and coiled around his tusks and crept toward his nostrils—

Emar opened his mouth and let out a tiny, muffled cry, revealing that the other cheese had transformed into a dark, crawling mass at the back of his throat.

"*God* in their Bodies!" yelped Elsyn. Her hands scrabbled unthinkingly at her sides, searching for something—*anything*—to help with, before finding a hard lump knotted in her shift. She picked at it, panicked, forcing her fingers into the knot, before it fell from her hip and hit the floor with a *clunk*: the tiny knife the goblins had given her.

She snatched it up and rushed forward. "Hold *still*," she said, grabbing Emar's crest and pulling his head back. She thumbed the sheath off the knife and swiped the blade at the fungus-like tentacles connecting the cheese to Emar's mouth.

The cheese *screamed* when the steel bit into it, emitting a sound like a wounded fox. The strands Elsyn cut went black and smoked; the others retracted toward the body of the cheese and Emar's mouth.

"Oh, *absolutely* not," she said, her stomach lurching upward. She thrust her tiny knife into the center of the vicious curd, and it squealed and deflated. "Petra, help, the other one is choking him—"

"Salt!" bellowed Hinat. They ripped off the top of a cask sitting near the door and seized a handful. "Keep his mouth open!"

As they hurried across the room, fist of salt clenched in front of them, the black, crawling things pushed out from Emar's mouth, dozens of tiny, sharp legs seizing the edges of his lips and sealing them shut. He whimpered and clawed at his face.

"I'm sorry," Elsyn said, shoving both her thumbs between his teeth and prying. After eleven years of milking, she had extremely strong hands, and the black legs stretched and hissed. Hinat slapped the salt against Emar's mouth, and the crawling thing bubbled and became less distinct. Elsyn pulled harder, and his mouth popped open. Petra, who had found a scoop among the shelves, poured a full cup of salt between his lips. The contaminated cheese crackled and foamed, but Emar could breathe again, and when Elsyn lowered him to the ground, he rolled onto his stomach and vomited the rest of the now-inert magic and the salt onto the ground.

Elsyn stood, panting. Very slowly she turned to Petra. "Why—*why*—why were those in *here?*" she demanded, her voice swooping high before she got hold of it. She took a deep breath, wiping her tiny knife on her shift, before bending to pick up the little leather sheath from where it had fallen. "That's fairy magic. It *reeks* of fairy magic. Why would you keep something that dangerous?"

The scoop in Petra's hands was shaking. "Talia only found them today. They were in one of the other cellars—we've had troubles with contamination—there's fairy magic coming through the floors in lots of places. The charms usually keep any problems contained, until we can take it out of the city to burn it."

Hinat was now pouring salt on the smear of vomit on the floor and the corpse of the cheese that Elsyn had stabbed. Emar sat with his back pressed against a cheese shelf, his arms wrapped around his knees, his tail wrapped around his feet. "So—sorry," he muttered, his eyes a little unfocused. "Didn't realize."

"'s all right," Hinat grunted. "Once you made eye contact with the cheese, it was all over."

"That's why we wanted the gate-tower as storage," Petra said. "It's close enough to the temple to—*discourage*—any magical infiltration, but far enough away for a good locking spell."

An image of the cheeses around her going soft and slimy, extending mucus-like tentacles over the shelves, oozing down the supports and across the floor, suddenly came to Elsyn, and she shuddered. "Why not move back into the palace temple? It needs some repair, but there's plenty of space—" She saw the expression on Petra's face and stopped speaking.

Thoughts crowded her head. Secluded inside the temple on the palatial hill, Elsyn had constructed an incomplete story of how the false Taryn had operated, corrupting everyone she touched, delegating the execution of her whims to her favorites. She had left scorched paths of destruction throughout the kingdom, empty temples, dead livestock, and nobles convinced of their own superiority to ordinary humans. But Oberon's daughter was dead, and fairy enchantments were still appearing in unexpected places, places that the false Taryn had never touched and which should have no residue of her presence. What had Algenymmar said? *There are many forces at work in the kingdom.*

No one but the goblins and I know that the real Taryn wasn't the one doing the corrupting, she realized, with a jolt of panic. And if my real sister who shares my blood had been consorting with fairies, I'd almost certainly be enchanted too, except—

"Fairies can't work on a god's ground," she said, exasperated, "and they don't have much luck with a god's consecrated priests, either. *You* know that. The High Priest ought to know that. *Who* thinks I've been put under a glamour?" But suddenly the answer was obvious. "Algenymmar. Oh. That was why she was so—the God in their Bodies."

"The Duke is very concerned," Petra said, sounding as if she was picking each word carefully out of a box of venomous snakes. "She has lost other people close to her to the influence of fairy magic. She is—not entirely rational about the matter."

And what, Elsyn wondered, did Petra mean by that? Surely not that *Ben* had been lured away by the fairies?

She opened her mouth to ask, but at that moment the box holding the contaminated cheeses jumped, as though there were a brace of hares trapped inside of it. Petra yelped and Hinat swore loudly, kicking clumps of salt at the box.

"I'm sorry," Petra said, "we really have to deal with this *now*—"

And she and one of the other priests were away up the stairs, carrying the box between them, Hinat stamping behind them with a scoop of salt in their hand.

On the third night of the second week of riding, Ben and Kandar made camp on a tall hill. Behind them lay a seemingly endless expanse of grass; before them, at the bottom of the hill, stood the edge of cultivated fields of wheat and barley. A narrow track among the grains would widen in another ten miles to a proper road, as Kandar recalled it.

He felt unbearably restless, his skin prickling with anticipation and anxiety. In the last hours of daylight, he had leaped down from the saddle and had raced Socks on all fours. It was not a game he could win fairly, and he skidded off the dimension just-up-and-to-the-left to keep up. He was not a skillful enough user of magic to break through into the goblin realm, so he bounced off and forward. It was exhausting, and he should have been exhausted, but the storm of emotions in his chest and belly seemed impossible to quell. Ben had laid a low fire and set the iron pot over it, but Kandar paced erratically in ever-widening loops around the horses, the coals, the grass, and the man. Soon he would be back in the city among his kin. Soon there would be Elsyn and all that she entailed: schemes to unravel, harm to be undone, a country to set to rights.

Soon there would be Elsyn. His encounter with her in the pasture and then in the temple cheesemaking room kept replaying in his brain, getting stuck again and again on certain details: her steady brown hands milking and holding a piece of cheese out to him; the lines of her muscular legs underneath the priest's shift; the funny quirk of her mouth up close.

Now there was Ben, and Kandar felt just as unsettled about that. His brain had likewise cataloged all of Ben's actions: the quick, precise movements of his knife as he cut plants for their nightly soup; the tender way he held Quince's head after taking off his bridle; the manner in which his dark eyebrows steepled toward each other when considering a hard question. Socks had given him an incoherent account of how Ben had rescued him, and now Kandar had those images in his head, too, of the big man moving surely and swiftly to cut his horse free.

It was very hard to behave himself. He wanted Ben to pay attention to him, and he found himself jumping over the fire, bunching his hind legs under himself to bounce from the ground to Socks' back and then down again, almost grazing Ben's shoulder with a hind claw.

"Here, now," Ben said, after the fourth such circuit, a note of exasperation coming through in his voice. "The night's not going to pass any faster. Calm down and come to bed."

Kandar, now sitting on his haunches on Socks' rump, considered this, eyeing Ben with speculative hope. "If you're offering," he said, without thinking.

Ben met his gaze solidly, annoyance and laughter warring in his expression. It took Kandar a moment to hear what had just come out of his own mouth, but Ben didn't look offended or enraged or frightened. He looked, if anything, interested, leaning forward, his dark eyes bright and his lips slightly parted.

The moment hung in the air. Kandar did not bounce from Socks' back to the ground, instead gingerly extending his long legs to the ground and standing up. Ben raised his eyebrows. Kandar walked toward him, all the fur on his body prickling.

Probably we should talk first, Kandar thought.

They did not talk first. He crouched in front of Ben and inhaled deeply. All the bristles in his crest stood straight up, and all the details of the night sharpened. He could feel the cool breeze over the grasses whip under his tunic and across his skin. He could see the glimmer of the dying coals reflecting in Ben's eyes and the faintest of smiles curving his lips.

His brain pulsed with smile-glimmer-smell. He turned his head and bit Ben's knee. His teeth went through the fabric of his trousers, and a startled laugh came from over his head. It was unexpected but appreciated when Ben bent his head closer and bit him back, hard, at the base of his jaw.

Let's have a bit of a wrestle, Elsyn's friend and I, he thought, friendly, wrestle, tussle, yes. His thoughts scrambled again: teeth, friend, bite, *want*. Kandar wrapped his right hand around the base of Ben's skull, to keep his face pressed against his neck. He fell back, pulling Ben down on top of him.

Ben came willingly, though he did not let his full weight fall on Kandar; the care of a large man used to dealing with smaller people, he thought. He had guessed from the rather proprietary expressions on several of the sea-goblins' faces that they had claimed Ben in more ways than one, but perhaps he still hadn't adjusted to the sturdiness of goblin frames.

Kandar felt exuberant. Ben smelled *excellent*, like horse and grass and goblin and sweat—

Ben grabbed both of his long ears to pull his head away from his neck, before leaning his face down and nipping Kandar's lower lip. A bite followed the nip, and then he sucked.

Kandar's brain clouded over entirely.

Ben lowered just his hips, grinding them against Kandar's with maddening slowness, enough to provide tantalizing pressure but no real friction through their clothes. Annoyed and delighted, Kandar folded his legs around Ben's waist and hung off him. The unexpected weight caused the large man to collapse on top of him with a soft *whuff* of breath. He was agreeably heavy.

Ben laughed and wrapped an arm around his back, rolling until Kandar was on top on him, straddling his hips. "I win, then," Kandar said out loud. His trousers were loose enough that his engorged cock had curved upward beneath them. He thrust himself vigorously against the noticeable lump below Ben's belt, and the other man let out another chuckle, before reaching behind Kandar with both hands and pushing down on his ass.

After a few minutes, Kandar panted heavily. Ben had gone red in the face and was sweating, but his eyes were half-closed and he was smiling with apparent enjoyment. Kandar abruptly pressed his nose below Ben's jaw again. Yes. He fumbled with the buttons on the neck of his shirt.

Ben, he saw, when he had pulled his shirt open, was nearly as furry as a goblin, with dark hair covering his massive chest and thick belly. "I've surprised the sea-goblins didn't offer to fight me when I said I was taking you away," he said, bending his head to snuffle in Ben's chest-hair.

A large hand came to the back of his head, rubbing his crest the wrong way and making frissons of electricity run up and down his spine. "It was a near thing."

Ben let him unbuckle his belt and unlace the cloth below it. His cock was proportionate to his body, and he was a very large man. Kandar took Ben in one hand, careful that his claws did not catch the thin skin there, and rubbed up and down. Ben turned his head to one side, breathing heavily. Kandar sat back on Ben's lovely, enormous thighs, stroking steadily now. Ben clutched his hands by his sides, and Kandar leaned down, pulling the skin down from the head and putting his mouth there.

Ben sat halfway up. "You—what—here—" Kandar stopped for long enough to grin hugely at him. The muscles of his torso clenched, and he gasped again. Kandar felt quite smug.

But Ben surprised him, reaching toward his trousers and tugging them open. He slid his hands up Kandar's backside, encouraging him to come up on his knees, and then he leaned all the way forward. He was very good with his mouth, good enough that Kandar was not able to warn him quickly enough, but Ben only laughed and wiped his face.

Some time later, they lay shoulder to shoulder. Kandar, quite out of breath, stared up at the spangled black of the sky. He had very much not considered the potential consequences of his actions, and he wondered uneasily if he would regret that later.

After a minute, without speaking or looking at each other, Ben rested his palm on Kandar's stomach, and Kandar placed his on Ben's.

PART FOUR

Once again, Elsyn found herself making cheese.

The sun had only just crested the horizon, but she hadn't been able to sleep. She couldn't lie down in the royal chambers without thinking about who had access to the palace and how easy it would be for the right person with the right pedigree to walk past the guards and find her unconscious. She thought, too, of the magic-contaminated cheese trying to strangle Emar. *There's fairy magic coming through the floors, in lots of places.* Ildar had told her that he and the witch Ashmallen had closed the fairy door Oberon's daughter had used to enter the palace. But how many other doors might here be?

After hours of pacing around the bed, the awful bed that her parents and the accursed fairy had slept in, she had walked up the dark length of the throne room and out into the pastures surrounding the temple. Her bunk in the dormitories was likely still vacant. There were no more than twenty priests left in the palace temple, down from the two hundred there had been in her childhood, and several of those remaining had private quarters not in the main temple building. Sleeping in the dormitory would be awkward and the thin mattress hard and scratchy, but it could not be worse than sleeping with the ghosts of betrayal and fear haunting the palace and the threat of creeping magic.

The dark, cold halls of the temple had not felt safe either. The same questions kept repeating themselves in her brain, about the High Priest and Neddie. They had unrolled so many plans to keep other priests safe and the temple machinery functioning, without breathing so much as a word to her. She, too, was a sworn dedicate of the Two-Bodied God; she had needed protection as much as the rest of them. Why had they abandoned her?

That left the barn wing of the temple, and she crept over the straw with whispered apologies to the dozing bovine forms humped across the floor. She had finally sagged into sleep propped up next to Turnip, who plastered her hair to her skull with a few drowsy licks.

She woke before sunrise to Cabbage's calf chewing her shift. It had seemed pointless to stay horizontal any longer and possibly be stepped on by an impatient cow, so she had risen, gotten the buckets, milked the three cows still milking, and started a batch of fresh cheeses. Whoever had done the milking last night had left a pail of now sharply acid milk in the dry sink in the cheese room, a piece of cheesecloth stretched over the top to keep out the flies. Yawning into her shoulder, she did mental calculations before shaking dried cardoon flowers out of a jar into the warming milk. The palace temple did not use lamb or calf rennet to coagulate the curd, though other temples sometimes did.

She felt sticky and itchy and a bit sick, so perhaps she could be forgiven for the first words out of her mouth when Kandar appeared in the door of the cheese room.

"Oh *no*. You're not supposed to be here."

He moved aside, and the man standing behind him stepped forward.

Elsyn raised the slotted spoon she had been using, then helplessly let it fall to her side.

She hadn't seen him in seven years. He was a little taller than he had been and much wider, his shoulders brushing both sides of the door frame. Dark hair touched his collar and bristled from his jaw. He didn't look very much like the boy who had hidden in store rooms and played crossing-string games with her.

He was alive.

"Ben," she said numbly. "I—you—but—Ben?"

He had come back.

"El—your Majesty," said the man in the doorway.

Elsyn's throat tightened. She widened her eyes, clutching the spoon, so she would not accidentally flick any stray bits of moisture down her cheeks by blinking. She wasn't ready for this. It had only been four weeks. She had thought she would have more time to find allies, to understand the temple network, to win Algenymmar and the High Priest over, to do anything except try and fail again and again. There had been no chance of him actually *finding* Ben, and yet here—

Where were you, she wanted to scream. Where were you all this time. Why did you leave. Why weren't you here when Taryn—when the imposter—when *that monster* was ruining everything. Why did you have to come back now, when I am exhausted and making a muck of everything.

And what if this was another fake? Perhaps Kandar had gone straight to the fairy kingdom to procure a changeling. Maybe Algenymmar was right, and Ben had been stolen away. The thought was painfully sharp, but the cold space it cut through her brain was welcome. She took a deep breath.

"Lord Albenyssar of Deragcaish," she said. "Welcome home." Her voice barely shook.

Ben bowed slowly, but his eyes remained fixed on hers. His expression was stony.

I would like some whey, came a familiar mind-voice from the hallway. I think you will agree that I did a very good job fetching this human for you, and therefore I deserve some whey. Just a bucket or two. You would barely notice it was missing.

"*Socks—*" That was Kandar's exasperated voice, but Elsyn would rather do anything than stare at Ben's unfamiliar familiar face, so she turned immediately, grabbed a ladle off a hook, and started dipping whey from the cheese vat into one of the empty milk buckets. She was damaging the new curd, but what did she care? The priests should be grateful there was any cheese at all. Who cared if the texture was bad. Who cared about anything at all.

She had to stop to wipe the hot tears off her face, and the bucket was only a third full when she whirled, shouldering rudely past Ben and into the hallway. Kandar stood there, holding the nose of Socks' harness and clucking softly.

"Here," she said flatly, letting the bucket drop to the stone floor with a *thunk*. She looked over, meeting Kandar's orange eyes and holding them for a moment. "You've done what I asked, so I suppose you're the one I'll marry. If you'll excuse me, I have to finish molding the cheese."

She turned on her heel and strode back to the vat of curds. She snatched the ceramic molds for the small fresh cheeses off the shelf, so violently that one of them bounced to the floor and shattered. From the hall, she heard the whinnies of Socks and another horse. Elsyn began to spoon curd into molds, as angrily as a human could manage to do that specific action, refusing to look up until she heard the sound of footsteps, human and equine, retreating away down the hall.

They had walked a scant two dozen steps back into the pasture before Kandar asked, "*Did* you tell Elsyn why you left?"

Ben felt so sick that the piece of fish he'd eaten for breakfast six hours ago was threatening to make another appearance. "I did not speak to her between when the body was found and when I departed."

"Did anyone *else* tell her anything?"

"How would I know that?" he snarled, rounding on Kandar. "Do you think the goblins receive couriers? Do you think I took a magic mirror with me so I might chat to my mother in the evenings?"

Kandar did not step back or even blink at his outburst. He only stared steadily back. One of his large, triangular ears twitched.

Ben felt pressure on his back; when he looked over his shoulder, Quince was there, leaning on him. He closed his eyes, and felt wet trickle over his cheeks. He felt his horse's soft nose whuffle his ear and hair.

He took a deep breath and forced his eyes open. Kandar was still there, his face unnervingly close. It had seemed safe enough, reasonable enough, to have a bit of fun with each other on the road, before diving back headfirst into the maelstrom of political and magical turmoil. He had felt so lonely, and Kandar, for all that he was taller and darker and sharper than the sea goblins, was a thread back to their safety, their trust. And—simple enough—he liked Kandar a great deal.

It didn't surprise him that Kandar had no qualms about trysting when he meant to marry Elsyn as soon as it could be managed. Ben had only spent two years training to be a captain before he had been banished, but that was long enough to know that soldiers made all kinds of arrangements among themselves when they were away from home. Many had a lover—or lovers—that their wives and families did not know about, or chose not to know about. He had known of a captain who had taken his camp husband, the company's quartermaster, home to his civilian wife and seven children for every festival month. He wondered, somewhat belatedly, what they had told her. But now—now Ben's duty was to Elsyn. He would do nothing that would shame her or make people question the allegiances of her consort.

This was not a helpful thing to be thinking about when Kandar's nose was six inches away from his. "I am sorry," he said. "That was rude. I don't know what Elsyn knows about my—my exile."

Kandar nodded, accepting the apology. "What about the rest of your family?"

"The rest of my—oh, gods." He had been so focused on getting back to Elsyn that he had not considered his duties to the house of Deragcaish. To the duke of Deragcaish. "I must tell my mother I have returned."

"Yes," said Kandar, and then, more slowly, "It is not widely known, what I told you about Taryn being taken to the fairy kingdom, and a false queen being left in her place. The goblins know, and Elsyn knows, and I could not say who else. The false Taryn made many friends who believed she would advance them and their families; they are not friends to Elsyn, or to me."

"Or to me," Ben said. He understood the implication, but he did not know how to explain the complicated prospect of his mother, who was friend to no one. "I will be careful. This game—this is the same game it has ever been, though the balance has been upset and the players moved without their knowledge." He reached up and stroked Quince's cheek, wishing he felt as full of bravado as he sounded.

We are good at games, Socks said suddenly. He had just returned from a sprint around the nearest pasture hillock, and now he stuck his nose in Kandar's ear and huffed loudly. We knocked Jolar off Pumpkin when we played polo. It was very funny.

"That isn't how you play polo," Kandar said, rolling his eyes upward and swatting the horse.

And then, without warning, he leaned forward, grabbed Ben's hand in his owned large, clawed one, and pressed his nose hard into Ben's cheek. It was a gesture the sea goblins used before going out to fish, and without thinking Ben responded in kind. His heart rate slowed.

"I will try to explain things to Elsyn," Kandar said, releasing Ben. "The goblin company sleeps in the lower palace; return there after you have met with your mother and we will plan."

Ben set his jaw. "Very well."

When Elsyn opened the door to the aging room, it hit something solid.

"Excuse me," she called. "You shouldn't stand ... " Her voice trailed off, as she saw that it was not a young priest standing in the hall.

Ildar bowed to her, a gray eyebrow lifted sarcastically. Jolar, standing to his right, also bowed. Kandar, behind them both, did not bow.

"You have to put Socks away," Elsyn told him. "Put him in one of the tall paddocks, where the young bulls stay when they're rowdy. I can't worry about whether he's going to break into the cheesemaking room."

"Is that where you keep the whey?" he asked.

"No, but it's where Socks saw it last. Where is—"

"All of our mounts have been stabled," Ildar interrupted crisply. "We have a wedding to plan."

Elsyn took a deep breath and nodded. After Ben had left, she had gone to the pump room and put her whole head under the icy stream of water, until she could no longer feel her cheeks, her lips, or her eyebrows. She had rebraided her hair and stolen a dusty priest's coat of undyed gray wool from one of the dormitory closets. It was big enough to fit her through the shoulders and hips but only fell to just above her knees, which made her think it had belonged to Roalsa, a massive, bluff woman who had been beloved by calves and young initiates alike. Roalsa, despite being in excellent health, had died of a heart attack two months after the false Taryn had been crowned. Her sister, Rononya, had disappeared soon after.

Now she met Kandar's eyes. All her limbs felt like jelly. She wondered if being married to someone meant you could pet the fur on his face. It looked very soft.

It would not do to be romantic or silly about this. She did not have better options. In fact, she had none. She would not let herself be used as a bargaining chip or a pawn by nobles who had delighted in the cruelty of the false queen, and that meant marrying quickly, to someone outside the court's influence.

Ben—

The very important fact about Ben was that he had chosen to leave her, and he had only returned because someone else had brought him.

"Yes," she said evenly. "Traditionally the monarch is married on midsummer day." There were a number of important religious ceremonies that accompanied such an event, which she supposed she would need to interrogate the High Priest about, if she could find them again.

"In a month," said Jolar thoughtfully.

"That's so *long*," Kandar said, dismay in his voice.

"That's so *short*," Ildar snapped. "I cannot imagine that a wedding can be arranged which befits our cousin's dignity in that amount of time."

"No, it can't. But I likely couldn't manage that if I had a whole year," Elsyn said frankly. "I told you. I have no allies from whom I can borrow money, and the false Taryn went through the royal coffers like a wildfire. Most of the gold is gone, and many of the estates that we took income from are now being managed by her favorites, who do not particularly care for my finances. I have asked to see their accounts. So far as they are concerned, none of the royal lands have had a successful crop or a good run of cheeses in five years." She had found this out from one of the palace stewards, who had cornered her, waving his ledger and demanding where he was to get the money to pay the wages of the three cooks, four scullery-maids, and two spit-boys under him.

"Well," Ildar said. He blinked.

"We should get married immediately, then," Kandar said. "Since there won't be a wedding to prepare." His eyes flashed when he said this, and Elsyn felt her face get hot. Kandar took a long step toward her, but Jolar elbowed him in the ribs.

"No. The ritual is important." And I need at least a month to prepare myself for this to really happen, Elsyn thought, panicky. It was one thing to be more or less comfortable asking Jolar to accompany her into the city to meet with some priests. It was quite another thing to imagine herself alone in bed with Kandar.

As Kandar followed Ildar and Jolar down a palace corridor, he felt a slight tug at his knee. He glanced downward. A large black cat sat there, an imperious claw hooked through the fabric of his trousers.

Jolar looked back down the hallway at him, eyebrows and ears raised, tail lashing, and he gestured at her to go on. When she and Ildar had descended a staircase out of sight, he turned to the cat.

"It would be better if we were not overheard," he said quietly.

The tom rubbed his massive head against Kandar's palm, turned, and strolled down a narrow side hall. Kandar followed: down, through a doorway on the left, up a staircase, and finally to a dusty, odd-smelling scullery. He inhaled deeply. It took several breaths to place the scent: an absence, rather than a presence. This tiny room was free of the residue of fairy magic.

He gave the cat an approving nod. "Wise fellow."

The cat stretched its jaw wide, yawning, and the king's voice, low and urgent, filled the space.

"Kandar—I am not telling you to do other than what you have already decided. I would not have sent you down into the human kingdom if I did not trust you to see clearly and act wisely. I only ask you to go carefully. Taryn is very young; Elsyn is even younger. They have been treated cruelly by those who should have protected them. They have been lied to by those who should have told them the truth. It will not be as simple as a wedding." The cat finished yawning and looked up at Kandar, cleaned a paw, then meowed. "Oberon and his daughter built walls around both Taryn and Elsyn, separating them from the reality of who they are and their place in the world. Inside the wall there are shadows and demons. It is not an easy place to enter, and you cannot save her from it."

His cousin's voice changed when he spoke the last sentence, becoming strange with grief.

The cat began to cough and hack, as though he had a hairball. The message is too long! Kandar thought. But he desperately wanted to hear the end of it.

"I could not do this alone. I am not enough, alone. *You* are not enough, alone."

The tom gagged and spat something on the ground that probably had once belonged to a mouse.

"Friend, come to me in the stables, and I will give you a roast pigeon," Kandar whispered, drawing a claw down the cat's back. The tom purred and closed his eyes.

Ben entered the ducal mansion through the servants' passage, a tunnel carved into the rock of the hill which came out several streets lower than the courtyard the house faced onto. The magic that kept the passage gate secure was very old and very strong, but—unfortunately for his mother, at least—it did not have a mechanism to disinherit direct descendants of the house's founder, even if they had brought disastrous shame upon the name of Deragcaish. He flicked a drop of blood from his thumb onto the moss growing over a stony retaining wall, and abruptly there was a doorway there, low enough that he had to duck to enter.

He had left Quince in the palace stables, in a stall between two goblin horses. It wasn't that he didn't trust his mother with his horse; it was that he couldn't be sure she wouldn't regard Quince as his accomplice.

The passage opened into a walled service courtyard at the back of the house. The steep slope of the hill meant that though only three stories faced onto the public plaza with the serpent fountain, six levels of windows stared down into this miserable little space. It felt like dozens of pairs of eyes behind those panes of glass followed his progress into the house.

He passed uneasily by the stairs to the lowest cellars, sunk even deeper into the hill. Their dark, low vaults had been a feature of his nightmares since earliest childhood. Other than a large cistern which she kept filled out of respect for the ancestors who had been besieged in an earlier version of this house, he didn't think his mother stored anything down there. Just past these was another stair, this one wide and shallow-stepped to accommodate servants rushing up and down carrying things.

He climbed past the floor where the regular store rooms were; then that of the lower, disused kitchens, dim and dusty, and finally, the third level, the new kitchens—

He walked into a meeting of fourteen priests and his mother, all standing around the scarred, massive table, except for two very old priests who were seated on stools at one end. Someone had spread out a map over its surface, weighting the corners with butter molds, but he couldn't see what region was depicted.

Ben, stunned by the number of religious persons in his mother's house and the seven additional years of age in her face, stubbed his toe and yelped. The priests jumped and whirled as one body to stare at the door.

Algenymmar, who had nerves of something denser and colder than steel, drew a line on the map and looked up.

"Good gods," she said. "I thought you were dead."

"As you can see, I am not," he said, then belatedly ducked his head to her. "My esteemed mother the Duke."

"Maybe it would be better if you were," she said flatly. "The assembled, my disgraced son Albenyssar."

The priests' heads, which had all turned to look at his mother, slowly swiveled back to look at him. Ben wondered if it were possible to combust under the weight of judgmental regard.

"The man the queen sent the goblin prince to retrieve?" piped up a brown young woman with black hair in tight ringlets.

His mother tried to her quell her with a glance, but the interrogatory spirit of the room had been awakened. "Have you met the goblins?"

"What's the prince like?"

"Was the queen serious when she said she'd marry him?"

"Will he be a good consort, do you think?"

"Can he run like a dog on all fours?"

"Did you kill the dragon?" This last was from one of the sharp-eyed octogenarians seated on a stool.

That was apparently too much for the duke. "Enough," she barked. "This meeting is adjourned. We will reconvene tomorrow."

One of the older priests looked like they would protest, but they met his mother's eyes and subsided. They inclined their heads to the duke and filed out, the two oldest supported by a younger priest on each side.

His mother shoved the butter molds to one side and rolled up the map before he could get a good look at it.

"Since when—" His brain was spinning with questions. "How long have you been hosting priests? What are you planning to do?" Another query came out of his mouth before he could stop it. "Have you been helping Elsyn?"

He had been so bewildered that he had not seen his mother move, but suddenly she was in front of him. She was a big woman—as wide and sturdy of frame as Elsyn, and moreover tall enough that she did not have to stretch to hit him across the face, which she did now. The slap resounded from the hard tile floors to the plastered vaults of the ceiling.

"Why are you here," she said, but it was not a question. "Why would you come back. Why would you think you were welcome in *my house*."

"I—" Ben said. His duty to Elsyn, his childhood friend and his queen, had carried him over the grasslands and past the wheat fields, through the city gates and up into the inner districts. The sense of imminent threat had let him push down the overwhelming shame of how he had left and why.

His mother had not forgotten. She had not been able to shove a saddle bag holding her clothes in their heraldic colors into the back of a cave and hide the knife and sword that bore the family crest beneath her mattress. He did not think any of the family retainers would have dared speak to her as Telwulf had spoken to him, telling him that he'd hatch an egg if he brooded any harder and ordering that he fish and herd goats with goblins for whom Deragcaish was nothing but a word, and a silly-sounding one at that.

Algenymmar, he realized, had not had a moment's respite from the knowledge that her son had ended her line and irreparably tarnished her family's honor in seven years.

The rage emanating from her body was like a physical force that hit him in the chest and forced him to step backwards.

"Do you think the fairies will elevate you as they elevated Taryn? I promise you, they will not. She stayed alive precisely as long as she was useful to them, and then they disposed of her as neatly as they got rid of that boy for you."

Ben, in spite of himself, gaped. "Mother—*what*—"

"Get out of my house," she said flatly. "Get out of here and don't let me see you again. I won't hide you and I won't lie for you."

Ben stared at her, his whole body numb. Then, without a word, he turned and went back down the stairs.

Fenar and Emar and a few of the other goblins had taken to sitting on the roof of the stables, to escape the gawking stares of the human grooms and converse unheard. Kandar thought about joining them, but he needed to think rather than talk. Being above the stench of human machinations and residue of fairy magic was enticing, though, and he did have a pigeon to catch.

After some searching, he found a disused courtyard tucked between two service corridors, the stone walls overgrown heavily with wisteria. The vines had thickened and gnarled, twisting upward like crooked hands swathed in green lace. He walked up to the roof as easily as if they were a staircase.

Kandar perched on a line of ridge tiles, staring out over the patchwork of different buildings that made up the palace. The mountains-just-to-the-left were more beautiful, safer, better-smelling, superior in every way to this cluttered pile of brick and stone, and the thought of leaving now was unbearable.

He had told Ben he would explain things to Elsyn, but that had been a very easy promise to make when staring into Ben's miserable face, and less easy to carry out when he thought of Elsyn's equally distressed countenance.

Different versions of this speech ran through his head: Your beloved childhood friend was taken in by the oldest fairy trick in the book, and as a result has spent seven years making an entire tribe of goblins fall in love with him. No, that probably wouldn't do. Your friend *and* his mother believed the word of an emissary from a country with no name, who was mysteriously easy to fall in love with, who died but left no body. .

.

Elsyn was no fool, and she'd seen the devastation wrought by a fairy through the power of suggestion. Oberon's daughter had used people's worst impulses against them, giving them permission to do things that they might have dreamed of but never would have carried out, had their better judgment not been clouded by her encouragement and a bit of magic. But it was one thing to believe that a fairy could have that power over members of hated families, who had always been vicious to Elsyn and her sister. It was quite another to understand that even the most honorable and decent could be twisted up in lies and fear, until they were unrecognizable. Kandar wasn't sure if his words were enough to explain that.

He wished he could talk to his cousin and ask the goblin king what he meant by entering a wall filled with shadows and demons. He had instantly liked the same things about Elsyn that he liked about Ben and Jolar. There was calm competence in her hands as she worked with the cheeses. The way she moved among the cows and spoke with Socks was always self-assured, always kind. She approached even terrifying things, like a room full of nobles who saw her as prey, with reserve and care. Compared to Taryn's occasional violent tantrums and haughtiness, Elsyn was delightfully pragmatic and straightforward.

Kandar thought of the third member of the partnership with his cousin and Taryn, the witch Ashmallen. They had been the king's sworn friend since Kandar was a child, and they had helped the king rescue him from more than one scrape. After one of these unfortunate adventures— when a raft of fairies had carried Kandar out over an ocean not in the goblin nor human nor fairy realms and dropped him, leaving him to tread water for days and struggle against lantern-eyed merfolk, who slipped up shadowy from below, seized his tail, and dragged him deep underwater, before he could struggle free and swim upward again—Ash had made up a charm for him. The spell was a bundle of the thinnest bird-bones and a spray of fragrant herbs which, when he wore it on a cord around his neck, settled his nightmares of teeth and fins and kept the sea from rushing into his mind at odd moments.

He liked Ash. They did not try to give him advice, and they, like Ben, could create wonderful food given a campfire and a pot. His cousin had told him that Taryn was almost calm around Ash, not so keenly aware of her own dignity that she was ready to sink her teeth into anyone who crossed her.

What would Elsyn be like, he wondered, if she could relax and trust him? Kandar thought of lying down with her in the grass, as he had with Ben; her black hair spread around her, a smile curving her lips, her dark eyes looking up at him. He would peel the priest's shift off of her, admire the curves of her breasts and belly, and stroke the muscles in her shoulders and thighs.

All his joints felt watery. This was not a helpful line of thought, he told himself sternly, unless he wanted to fall off the roof.

An unwise pigeon fluttered down onto the gutter below him, and Kandar jumped. The bird had time for a panicked beat of its wings before he seized it in one hand and snapped its neck with the other.

That was the cat taken care of, he thought, shoving the pigeon head-down into his belt. Now to talk with Elsyn.

Elsyn had successfully avoided being alone with Kandar for three days. There was now a strange light in his eyes whenever he looked at her, a gleam made her think of Daffodil the bull when the gate to his paddock was ceremonially opened each fall.

Perhaps it was only down to being extremely busy. The wedding would not be as elaborate as a royal wedding ought to be, but a great number of people still had to be informed of places and times and reminded of obligations. After talking with several of the stewards who had kept the palace accounts—and wept over them, during the years the false Taryn sat on the throne—Elsyn thought that at least two of the families who had been given royal properties as favors could be badgered into giving them back, in the guise of wedding gifts. A little bit of cash income would make her position much easier. The temples had been operating entirely on barter for the past three years, Petra told her, which was well enough for getting aid to farmers whose livelihoods had been wiped out by the cattle plague, but not particularly helpful for paying palace staff or soldiers.

Elsyn's lack of knowledge of the palace guard had quickly revealed itself as a serious liability, as crowd control was not something that could simply be waved away when thousands of people were expected to jam into the courtyard before the city temple to watch the wedding ceremony. The army was another problem altogether. In her grandfather's time, when there had been invasions from across the great southern sea, a standing body of soldiers had been trained and garrisoned in the lower city. Elsyn's mother, however, had let the garrison empty out, and by the time the false Taryn was crowned, the infantry was a shadow of what it had been. More troubling, several of the nobles had maintained their own private forces of fighting men—Glascrann, for one, and another family who rarely entered the capital, the Tordove.

"You'd do best to train up some of your own soldiers, even if they're part-time conscripts," Jolar told her. "Start by teaching them to fight fairy monsters, like the ones that come down the goblin road."

They stood together in the guard tower of the priest-gate with Amlar, Petra, Hinat, and two other priests, Grania and Tircia. Both women were from near the capital and looked very much like Elsyn, with waving black hair, curved noses, and shoulders like oxen. A table had been brought up, and Petra had unrolled a map of the city and surrounding area on it, drawn on a piece of linen in black ink. With Grania's help, she had marked locations of recent strange events with a piece of red ochre. Most of these were rogue cheeses, though some were reports from shopkeepers and street cleaners of weird beasts they'd found in gutters and cellars.

"So you think that any place there's a *lot* of weird things going on, there might be a fairy door still open nearby," Elsyn said to Amlar.

She shrugged. "It would make the most sense. Fairies can push through the skin between worlds anywhere, but it's easier if there's already a hole."

The priests in the room all shuddered and made gestures of god-calling.

"This is something new, if they're keeping the doors open for longer," Jolar said thoughtfully. "There are places naturally full of holes, like the marshes and the dark forest. But in the mountains, usually a fairy door opens for a night, or a season, and then closes again. I thought it was the same in the human realm."

Elsyn stared at the rash of red marks on the map, dispirited. There was a cluster around the palatial hill, mostly to one side. "And all of these are in the last two months?"

Tircia squinted at the map. "To the best of my recollection. There was less weird stuff, before," added. "When *that one* was on the throne."

Grim looks were exchanged across the table. It's not yet a coordinated attack, thought Elsyn. But it might become one. Jolar's idea of training citizens to fight monsters sounded better and better.

"How many maps like this do we have so far?" she asked Petra.

Petra looked to Hinat, who said, "At least twenty, but mostly for towns in the south. None of *her* people hold as much land there, and it's easier for priests to move about. There aren't nearly so many problems down there with the cheese, but more than I'd like."

The sound of boots on the stair made Elsyn's head jerk up. "Who —"

"That will be Ben," Jolar said. "I asked him to come have a look."

"Oh," Elsyn said. "Yes. Of course." Her stomach did a jig and then somersaulted into her chest when the broad-shouldered silhouette filled the door.

"Your Majesty," he said, bowing to her and nodding to each of the priests in turn. Petra turned to Elsyn, grave apprehension in her face.

"This is Albenyssar of—this is Ben," Elsyn said. Grania's eyebrows went up, and Hinat frowned.

"Can he be trusted?" they asked, voice sharp. "I have heard—"

Elsyn's throat ached, and for a moment she was without words. She focused hard on the map but didn't really see it.

"The prince Kandar will vouch for him," Jolar said, in a tone that had a sword behind it. "I do not know what you have heard."

"What's this?" That was Ben's voice, and Elsyn felt him step up to the table next to her.

Petra explained, with a lot of hand gestures. Elsyn couldn't look at Ben's face, but she saw his fingers twitch when the phrase *strangler cheese* was uttered. She wished she could laugh, but it would probably come out as a sob. "Have you made inquiries about fairy magic in the rest of the kingdom?" he asked.

Elsyn took a deep breath. "Yes. Several priests are drawing up maps and marking down what we already know on them, and those going out to distribute food have been charged with questioning the farmers." Pride, both in having a plan and keeping her voice even, eased the tightness in her throat a little.

Ben's hands appeared in her field of vision, as he braced his arms on the table and leaned over the map. "There may be incursions that happen far from settlement," he said. "Kandar and I encountered a fairy trap in the grasslands on our return."

"What sort of trap?" Jolar demanded.

"It's hard to describe. The grass had become ... alive, not as a plant but as an animal, and it took hold of his horse. It would have dragged him into the ground if we had not fought it off."

"Could they set that kind of trap here, in the city?" asked Tircia.

The priests stared at the goblins. The goblins stared at the priests. All of them turned to stare at Elsyn.

"Can Ildar close a fairy door, if we find one?" she asked.

Amlar and Jolar glanced at each other. "He may need assistance," Amlar said cautiously. "And he probably can't keep them from opening new ones."

Grania looked at the sliver of sky visible through the arrowslit. "We'd best go," she said. "The cows will want milking soon. We will send word when we've filled out the maps for the region around the city."

They had not shared with Elsyn where they were hiding the cows that gave the milk for the cheeses they were bringing into the capital. She still thought that probably meant they were on one of the Deragcaish estates, and Algenymmar or the High Priest had sworn them to secrecy.

The priests filed out. Petra made as if to roll up the map, but Elsyn stopped her. "I'll give it to you tomorrow. I need to think on this a little more."

Petra looked at Ben, at Elsyn, again at Ben. She clearly didn't want to leave the map, and she clearly didn't want to say why she didn't want to leave it.

"It will stay with me, and I will keep it safe," Elsyn said.

Petra's eyes moved once more between the two of them. "You're Algenymmar's son."

"Yes," Ben said quietly.

I asked Kandar to bring him back, Elsyn thought. I wanted him— I wanted him *here,* whatever the reason he had for leaving. They shouldn't doubt him because of me.

She opened her mouth to say something—she wasn't sure what— only to be cut off by Petra.

"Elsyn," she said, "do *you* trust him?"

It was such an odd question to ask, and Elsyn answered without thinking. "Yes, with my life." It was, she reflected tiredly, the truth. Every part of her body hurt when she thought about being abandoned—not abandoned, she snapped at herself, it wasn't as if he had sworn fealty to her seventeen-year-old self—left by Ben, but he must have had a good reason. If she had been given a chance to escape the capital, maybe she would have taken it too.

Petra nodded slowly. "All right." She glanced at Ben one last time, then nodded to Elsyn and left.

Elsyn stared down at the map, puzzled. Hinat might have questioned Ben so sharply because they didn't know he was, but Petra recognized him. Elsyn thought Petra might have even met Ben before, during one of the few times he had managed to sneak himself into the temple after she had been initiated. What were the priests worried about?

The cluster of red dots around the palace caught her eye again, and she bent closer, trying to match up each one with her memory of the city. There were three on the goldsmiths' street, and another in the cut flower district.

"Do you remember what this one was?" she asked, pointing to the dot just next to those three. "Was it a cheese or a creature?"

The room was silent. She looked up and realized that the only person left at the table with her was Ben; the goblins had left with the priests.

Elsyn breathed deeply through her nose. This had to happen sometime, she thought. "Do you know what street this is?" she asked. "I can't place it."

Ben studied the intersection of lines at the tip of her finger. "I think it's the quarter of the water-pumpers."

"That one was a creature," she said, remembering Tircia's description. "A lizard with fourteen legs." She sighed. "Maybe we should have marked the problems with the cheeses in a different color. Some of these are just very strange molds."

"How would you know? Aren't all cheeses moldy?" He sounded curious.

"There are molds which are good and friendly, molds which are expected but not delicious, and molds which ruin the cheese completely," Elsyn said. "And now there are apparently weird fairy molds with eyes that follow you around the room and blink a lot."

This was good, she told herself. She was getting used to Ben again, used to talking like a normal person and not like an injured, terrified child.

Then he reached past her to touch another place on the map, his fingers brushing the side of her hand, and the unexpected contact surprised her into jerking away. He slowly lowered his arm to his side, and she looked him in the face, suddenly ashamed. "I didn't mean—" He turned his head a little, and she noticed a change in his profile. "When did you break your nose?"

Ben touched the bridge of his nose reflexively. "It's been a few years. Telfar didn't—it was an accident on a boat. With a sail. Hitting me in the face."

"You've been at sea?" Elsyn asked.

"Not exactly," Ben said.

The enormity of the seven years he had lived without her unrolled between them.

Elsyn looked away first. "What were you pointing out on the map?"

"It was—I was—I—only that these three dots are all close to a house owned by Iuliud Glascrann." He pointed to a cluster up the street from the goldsmiths. "He is my mother's neighbor, and was a great favorite of—*her.*"

Does he know that it wasn't Taryn, all these years? Elsyn thought, a bubble of panic in her chest. She didn't think she could make her mouth say those words into the thick air of the room.

"Do you think you could talk to the palace guard about the wedding?" she blurted. "There ought to be a few dozen standing about, herding the crowd away from sharp corners and stamping out fires."

Ben went oddly still. "They would take orders better from their queen."

"They wouldn't," Elsyn said, "because I'm scared to death of them." That was too honest, and her face reddened.

She felt Ben looking at her, but she couldn't meet his eyes. The guard room, already stuffy on a summer day, was rapidly approaching suffocating.

"Has Kandar spoken with you?" Ben asked.

"About what?" she hedged.

"About—about all this," he said, gesturing at the map. It was clearly not what he had meant.

"I will ask him," Elsyn said, glad to have a reason to escape this painful conversation. She rolled up the map and tucked it under her arm. "Good day, Albenyssar."

Kandar finally found the black tom asleep on a water butt outside the stables. "I've a gift for you," he told the cat, crouching to look him in the eye. "Not roasted, but I've been busy."

Another cat slept next to the black one, an orange tabby halfway out of kittenhood. It stretched and yawned when he offered his hand to the tom, then got to its feet with interest when he produced the pigeon, considerably worse for wear after three days jammed in his belt. The feathers the black cat plucked from the bird's body distracted the kitten, and it tumbled to the ground in pursuit of a fluttering primary. The tabby got up, shook itself, and pounced on the feather—or where the feather had been, until Kandar tugged it away. It flattened its forequarters against the ground and wiggled its haunches, in preparation for a mighty leap onto his knee. The feather was suddenly not as interesting as the light flashing off a metal button on his pocket. Kandar delicately pried the kitten's teeth out of the fabric, and it mewed pitifully.

"Kandar," said the king's voice from its mouth, "be wary. The wedding contains a powerful god-rite, and it does not suit Oberon that it shall happen."

He lifted the kitten to eye level, giving it a severe stare, and it swiped at his nose.

"Ask him if he's got any advice for making Elsyn talk to me," he told it irritably. "Otherwise tell him he can bite his own tail."

When he set the cat down, it sat and cleaned one paw, apparently uninterested in delivering his message. One paw tidy, it switched to the other, taking special care with the fur between its toes.

I have three weeks, he told himself. There must be a moment when she's not meeting with someone or making cheese or asleep.

"I need to talk to you," Elsyn's voice said.

Kandar blinked up at her. She'd just stepped out of the stable door next to the water butt, and the orange cat hurled itself upon the hem of her linen shift. Elsyn scooped up the little animal in one hand, giving him a very agreeable view of her shapely calves as she unhooked four tiny claws.

"Don't do that," she said shortly, sitting down on a mounting block shoved against the wall. She cradled the cat in her elbow.

"What?" he said.

"Don't stare at my legs."

"Why not?" he said, adrift. Was this a human rule he didn't know about?

"I know I look—I know I'm great deal larger than most humans," she said stiffly. "I don't enjoy being reminded constantly."

The black tom made an offensive crunching noise as it ripped off the pigeon's leg. Kandar considered Elsyn's statement for a minute before deciding that no amount of consideration was going to make it more comprehensible. "*What?*"

"That's not what I need to talk to you about."

"You can't get angry with me for something and then not explain why," he said. "That's a human thing, holding grudges you won't admit to. Explain."

Elsyn now looked at bewildered as he felt. "Obviously—I mean —I'm not—" She took a moment and collected herself. "It would be one thing if I were a farmwife or a regular priest in a village temple," she said quietly. "I'm strong. I can move even the big cheeses, the ones that weigh as much as grown man. And it's no bad thing to be big when you're handling cattle. Onion bullied some of the initiates, but she never tried it with me."

"Onion the cow?" Kandar said. He understood all of the individual words she had used, he thought, so why on earth couldn't he follow what she was talking about?

"Yes. I think—I think if I had been born as someone who only *did* things, who didn't have to be a symbol that people *looked* at, it wouldn't have mattered so much that I—that I—" She stuttered to a stop, before struggling on. "My mother looked like a queen. Taryn—well—*she* looked like a queen. Slender as a deer, pale as the moon, beautiful as a myth. Even people who hated her said that. If you had to dress me up in silk and jewels, I'd look like a sausage stuffed in a casing with fennel seeds poking out." This last sentence was delivered with the bitter conviction of a prayer she had been forced to say over and over again. "That's all. I know what I am, and I don't want to think about it."

Kandar's jaw worked in outrage, but she rushed on before he could interject. "It's about Ben. Everyone's acting like something's wrong with him—his mother and the priests—and I don't—" Abruptly she shoved the heel of her hand into her left eye, but he could still see the tears leaking from her right. The orange cat was now resting on her breast, half-asleep. He eyed its comfortable position enviously. All of this would be much easier if Elsyn would let him get that close. "People have been keeping things from me for *eleven years*," she choked out. He thought she was more furious and overwhelmed than sad.

He reached over and stroked the kitten's head, wishing very much he could pet her instead. "I can tell you what Ben told me," he said.

"I'm going to kill her," Elsyn said to Turnip. Given that she was about to commit a homicide, she felt weirdly calm. "I'm going to walk into her house and shake her until she apologizes, and then I'm going to push her out a window."

BEST NOT SMELL BURNING GRASS, Bean warned, from her other side.

Elsyn had not asked Jolar or any of the other goblins to accompany her. When Kandar was done speaking, she had stood up, thanked him, bowed, and walked straight to the temple pasture to collect her cows. Turnip came, as did Bean, and after a minute two of the herd not in milk, Asparagus and Leek, joined them.

They left by the newly-functional priest-door, marching down the cobblestone way, through the goldsmiths' street, and up the narrow street that led to the courtyard of the serpent, surrounded by noble houses.

This time, Algenymmar did not appear preemptively from the portal of the Deragcaish mansion. Elsyn lifted her hand and pounded on the door. I am not going to shout at her, she told herself. I am not going to shout. I am going to go in and demand what in all the names of the Two-Bodied God is *wrong* with her and what has rotted her brain into soft cheese, but I am not going to shout.

The smaller door creaked open, and a harassed-looking priest who she vaguely recognized, dressed in red Deragcaish livery, poked her nose out. "What can I help you—oh, Elsyn—oh, *your Majesty*—"

"Open the gate," Elsyn ordered. "The cows come in with me."

This priest was a round woman, curly black hair going to gray. She stared at Elsyn for a minute, her mouth agape. Bean shook her head, and the tips of her massive horns whistled through the air. Asparagus mooed loudly.

The priest disappeared, and the gate creaked open.

Elsyn met Algenymmar coming down the marble stairs which approached the formal parlor. The older woman's face was white with fury.

I will not shout, Elsyn thought.

"How dare you enter my house without invitation," Algenymmar said, rage making her voice crack. Her hand clutched at the pommel of the knife in her belt.

"How could you think he had killed an innocent person?" Elsyn said, in what she thought was a very reasonable tone. It struck her, listening to the echoes of her words die away through the house, that it might seem less reasonable to other people.

Leek nosed over an end table at the bottom of the stairs. It fell to the floor with a crash.

Algenymmar had gone still, her face frozen, her chest rising and falling in great heaving breaths.

Leek pulled the drawer out of the end table with her tongue and began to nose through its contents.

"I will not discuss this with you," Algenymmar said. If she had spoken with that depth of contempt to Elsyn when she was child, she would have crumpled to the ground and wept.

Elsyn, who stood three stairs below the Duke, holy cattle behind her, linen shift wrinkled, hair wrapped in an untidy braid around her head, incandesced.

"You sent your only child into the wilderness to die or be killed, because of a false accusation. You were willing to end your own line rather than argue for the truth." She was definitely shouting now, because otherwise she couldn't hear her own words over the thundering of her heart. "I have spent my whole life thinking you were more honorable, more *decent,* than my parents, because you saw the truth of the people they surrounded themselves with. You did not pretend Taryn was anything but a monster. You did not turn against the temple, even when it would have served you to do so."

"And how do you think the temple would have trusted me, if I had damned your sister's crimes, but made sure my own son faced no consequences?" snarled Algenymmar. Her face shone wetly, and after a stunned moment Elsyn realized she was crying. "They saw what your mother did too, how she let her child become a tyrant. I am not above the gods' law. My family is not above the gods' law."

Elsyn, who had thought her rage was calming, felt it roar back to life. "The law is not meant to punish innocent men. The law is meant to find out the truth."

"Do you think it matters what the truth is, if no one believes it?" Exhaustion and bitterness warred in the Duke's voice.

"It matters because Ben is *your son,*" Elsyn said. Probably she would only be able to whisper tomorrow. "You owed him better than this."

HERD IS ALL, Bean said sternly from the bottom of the stairs.

"You have no idea what the last seven years have been like," Algenymmar hissed. "Do you want to know how many priests she killed? Do you want to know how desperate your people have been for help? There was a drought before the cattle plague. There might have been grain in the palace, but there was none in the countryside."

Elsyn looked into her black eyes. "I am sure Taryn was be delighted that she succeeded in convincing you to throw away your son, with hardly an effort on her part," she said. "And she would be happier yet to know that you deny your legitimate queen."

Over Algenymmar's shoulder, a familiar, narrow face appeared, eyes stretched wide in panic—the High Priest, standing at the top of the flight of stairs. They looked at Elsyn and then back up the stairs, clearly torn.

I don't have any anger left for them, Elsyn thought, disgusted, and turned to leave.

Ben had taken to sleeping in the goblin quarters in the lower palace. He had not objected when Kandar had slipped into his room and curled up on his feet like a very large, very angular cat. A few mornings Kandar woke him by nuzzling into his neck. Only once had this led to any further tussling. The crushing atmosphere of the palace, the accumulated fear and suspicion and neglect, left Ben cold and queasy. He worried constantly about Elsyn, even knowing that she slept with the holy cows and that Jolar sent a different pair of goblins to patrol the temple pastures every night.

Ben had hunted up the remaining captains of the palace guard and discussed the wedding with them and how many guards would be needed where. All three of the men were weirdly reluctant to follow basic orders. He couldn't tell whether the guard had been corrupted by the false queen or whether they were now in pay of one of the other noble families, but he suspected both. The guard barracks were adjacent to the noble apartments, and they were suspiciously well-appointed, compared to the general disrepair of the rest of the palace. It would not take very much money, he thought, to buy Elsyn's safety from any of them.

None of the three captains he spoke with forgot themselves so far as to demand where he'd been, but he saw the question in their faces. One had clearly heard something when Ben had been banished; he could barely keep the sneer off his lips. The other two were worried and watched him with sharp eyes.

They want to know whether Elsyn has plans for retribution, he thought grimly, as he walked back to the lower palace. I wonder how many priests they helped Taryn—the false Taryn—get rid of.

He had reached a hallway by one of the lower kitchens when an odd pair confronted him. Kandar crouched on the ground in front of a small gray cat with white socks and a white bib. His tail lashed as he murmured continuously to the small animal, who sat still and stared at him, for all the world like it was listening carefully. He finished speaking, clasped his hands, and bowed his head to the cat. The cat stood, rubbed its head on his proffered hands, and walked through a doorway out of sight.

"What are you doing?" he asked curiously.

"Sending a message to my cousin," Kandar said. "Did the sea-goblins never ask cats to carry tales?"

Ben considered this, as Kandar stood and dusted off his trousers. "Once or twice Telwulf caught a seagull and told it to take a message back to the caves, when the eeling boat was blown far off course."

"There you are," Kandar said, falling into step beside him.

"What do you tell your cousin of human affairs?" Ben asked.

Kandar was silent for a long time, and Ben wondered if he'd somehow offended him. Finally he said, "Do you think Elsyn is beautiful?"

The question felt like a punch to the gut. He thought of the Elsyn who had stood over the map in the tower, level-headed, careful, discussing her plans—sensible, well-thought-out plans—with priests and goblins. Noticing other things about her—her thick dark hair escaping its braid; her well-formed lips and how often they twitched with humor; and, worst of all, the heft and curve of her adult body—had felt like a betrayal of the other Elsyns he had known: the sixteen-year-old, rigid with rage and grief at her parents' funeral; the twelve-year-old wringing out her skirts after falling into a fountain; the five-year-old, her sleeping head on his shoulder as he carried her back to the royal apartments from some Taryn-led adventure. He had been eight; he could still carry Elsyn comfortably when he was eight.

"I have known her a long time," he said. "Do you ... find her beautiful?"

In two weeks, Kandar was going to lie down with Elsyn as her husband. Cold seeped through his veins with that knowledge. If Oberon's daughter had never come, I might have married Elsyn, he thought. Probably, even. I would have made her a good husband, if things had been different.

The cold feeling wasn't envy, he realized. It was grief.

He realized Kandar watching him with eyes narrowed. "Yes? What?"

"I was hoping you'd notice it was a stupid question, but you just asked me the same thing again. Did Oberon's daughter infect your brains somehow? Elsyn is glorious. If I'd known she was here, I would have come down from the mountains years ago. She looks more like a queen than anyone I've ever seen, and my mother hunted gods. Minor ones," he amended, after a moment.

They entered the stables. Quince lifted his head from the hay rack and whinnied softly. Ben rubbed the horse's soft nose. Kandar's last sentence made understanding click into place. "That line of thinking started before the false Taryn came," he said. "Though I'm sure she continued on what others had started. Elsyn's mother was ... no, I shouldn't say that. But she did not ..." His voice trailed off. "I don't think I can explain with going into years of history between Elsyn's mother and my own."

"So it's a generational madness," muttered Kandar. "Wonderful."

At that moment, Socks arrived in the stable with a cacophony of snorting and stamping of feet. Did you know there's an entire room full of snacks just up those stairs? he demanded of Kandar. Why didn't you tell me before?

"Do you mean the *kitchens?*" Ben asked, both amused and horrified.

The red-faced cooks who piled through the stable door at this moment confirmed this assumption, and he turned to placation.

The wedding would happen the next day. Kandar felt like he might chew his leg off, or at the very least a foot.

After some refinement to remove less significant events and identify which cheeses had been stored longest in which location, Petra's maps still showed some new source of fairy magic between the palatial hill and the hill of the noble mansions. Kandar had taken to patrolling that area of the city at night, hunting for the smell of fairies. Hopefully none of the city dwellers noticed their soon-to-be prince-consort sniffing around their back gardens in the darkness. Jolar went with him some evenings, though he suspected this was to stop him from breaking into likely-smelling cellars.

There were alarming reports from the countryside, especially in the towns near the goblin road in the northeast. Ildar had spoken privately with Kandar. He meant to ride north with as much information as they had soon after the wedding.

The gray cat had come back with his cousin's answer over the course of several nights, rewarded each time with soft cheese. The first bit of advice Kandar suspected actually came from Ash, consisting of when he ought to serve Elsyn cheesy toast with jam to soothe her nerves (mornings, mid-afternoon, and whenever he noticed that Elsyn was struggling to think clearly.) Two more evenings were spent detailing which cheeses went with which jams and how long to grill the toast. The second batch of suggestions were most definitely from the goblin king himself and consisted of actions which would be difficult to carry out in public, unless he didn't mind embarrassing a lot of priests.

On the sixth evening, the voice that came from the cat was not his cousin's. Kandar's head jerked sharply, and he stared at the animal. "You can't tell her anything," Taryn said. "The more you argue with her, the more she'll dig in her heels. Say what you mean, then back off and let her think about it." A pause. "Be kind, and she'll come around to you."

The cat took the rest of the cheese and walked off. Kandar pulled on one and ear and looked at the late sunlight slanting across the stone floor. The message had come early today. It seemed like a poor choice to go hunting fairies the night before his wedding, and in any case he wanted to do nothing more than talk to Elsyn.

She was at the entrance to the temple barn, bent over a calf trapped between her legs. One of the cows, white dappled with red, one horn missing its sharp tip, stood nearby, commenting anxiously on Elsyn's progress.

"Whoever you are, I could use some help," she called, without looking up. "This little man is very wiggly, and I need to clean this foot."

Kandar grabbed the calf's forelegs. When Elsyn stepped aside, he picked him up and sat him up on his haunches. The calf did not much like this and yelled.

"Thank you," she said, to Kandar, and, "Don't you start," to the calf. She produced a small knife from her shift—goblin-made, he noticed with interest; it must have come from the small store of gifts they had brought with them—and scraped the mud off one of the calf's hooves.

"Is he lame?" Kandar asked.

"A little bit. I can't tell if it's a rock stuck between his toes or an abscess. Pumpkin, hush, I'm not murdering your baby."

Pumpkin did not seem sure of this, but another calf romped by and head-butted her udder, drawing her attention.

"How do you do this with one of the big cows?" Kandar asked.

"All the holy herd will give me their feet to clean," Elsyn said absently, prying a dark object free from between the calf's toes. "There's a chute for visiting cattle behind the temple, but it needs repairs. "

"On the list," he muttered.

"On the list," she agreed. She flossed the hem of her shift through where the rock had been, cleaning out more dirt and debris. "His foot is still a little raw, but I think it will heal. You can let him down."

The calf, indignant, shot away from them as soon as he was unhanded.

Kandar looked at Elsyn. The setting sun made the skin on her shoulders and forearms glow. All of the advice his cousin and Ash and Taryn had given him slid out of his brain like it had never been there.

"The wedding can't get here soon enough," he said, fervently.

"It will be good to have it over with," Elsyn said, cleaning her small knife with a handful of grass.

"It will be good to be with you," he said, and she looked up at him.

"I hope so," she said, and there was a complicated mix of emotions in her voice that he could not pick apart. "I am glad—I am glad to marry you. You will be a good prince-consort." She looked away again.

"I am glad you are queen," Kandar said meditatively.

"Really?" Elsyn sounded doubtful.

"Yes. I would have asked you to take me the first day I saw you if you had been only a priest who makes cheeses and herds cows; but I do not know how to make cheese, and I am not good with cows. I would followed you around and annoyed you very much. But you are queen, and you need someone who can go on quests and fight and smell out fairies, and those are all things I am good at."

Elsyn gaped at him.

Kandar's tall silhouette moved away from her through the shadowy grass, and Elsyn stared after him. After a minute she noticed her mouth was still open, and she closed it.

Kandar crested a hillock and then plunged down into a grass gully.

Abruptly a cow blocked his path—not the mountainous red bulk of the Boss Cow, Bean, but a white-and-red dappled beast of a slightly more delicate build. Her horns were no less massive, though, and each one ended in a sharp black tip.

He shifted to the left. She swung her head to follow him. He dodged to the right; she turned her whole body to stop him again. The path here had been carved deep into the dirt by generations of bovine foot traffic, leaving two shoulder-high walls of earth to either side of them. He thought he could probably jump over a normal cow, but he felt uneasy about his chances with a god-touched one.

So he sat back on his haunches and eyed her. "How may I serve you, O lady?" There was a specific vocabulary of body movements and words to approach a noble horse, and he suspected this held true for holy cattle as well.

The cow swished her tail. Her voice was not so loud nor so clear as Bean's; the meanings were difficult to pick out from rustling of the grass and the flickering of shadows moving across the ground.

Her name was Turnip, and she was four summers old. Her dam was Onion, and her best friend was Squash. This information was conveyed in images, smells, vibrations, and a sense of different plants moving through her body. All cows were hallowed to the Two-Bodied God, who was human and cow and earth and fungus and many other things. The God allowed them to speak clearly to some humans, and some humans to speak clearly to them.

Kandar was fascinated in spite of himself. He knew some of the horse-lore, but it had not occurred to him that cows had their own faith as well.

Turnip threw her head, and Kandar had to jump back to avoid being brained by a gigantic horn. She wasn't sniffing to itch her nose, she told him severely, and her tone was sharp and clearer than it had been. He needed to pay attention.

Turnip knew what humans were like, and she knew what gods were like, and she knew there was something *other* than those which was in the kingdom now. Before Elsyn had become the Boss Cow of the humans, there had been a funny smell that hung around the palace all the time, a smell like white flowers and moldy hay and sour milk. Bean had kept all the cattle away from non-priest humans then, but Turnip had been a curious calf and a curious heifer. She had made many clandestine trips down into palace, trying to locate the source of the smell and poke it if she could.

The image she showed Kandar next made him grimace and bare his teeth. From a cow's perspective, the false Taryn's disguise had not been very good. Her smell was terribly wrong, and her hide pattern had abruptly changed, from brown on the head and arms and light brown on the body to white all over. Only the black hair was correct. The insect woman had smelled like bad grain and lilacs, Turnip told him. The place where Elsyn had been knocked down by shadowy men also smelled like this.

"Yes," Kandar said, confused, before demanding, *What?*

The next set of pictures and smells were even harder to parse. A cow's eyes are set on the sides of her head, so most of her vision is peripheral, and her depth perception is limited to a small patch directly in front of her face. Kandar also suspected that whatever magic allowed Turnip to *sneak* distorted the distances around her.

Pay attention! Turnip repeated, sounding angrier and—afraid?

Kandar took a deep breath and allowed her remembering to wash over him.

Elsyn was in front of the cow in this memory, just ahead across a paved space, with walls rising on either side. Next to her was another woman, who smelled like paper and dust. They were outside, next to a stone wall covered in ivy. Turnip, in her memory, considered a snack, then decided against it. The air was cool and dark. An oil lantern some distance away cast its smoky odor and limited light a few feet on all sides, reflecting off the street and the walls.

The light went out. For a moment Turnip could not see, and neither could Kandar, immersed in her memory. One set of footsteps echoed around the space, running toward Elsyn; then another, then another. The cow plunged out of her hiding spot, trotting toward the smells of sweaty male human and naked metal. Voices echoed through the night. Elsyn shouted and then was cut off. Turnip did not understand human speech, but Elsyn's tone had been distressed. Kandar felt Turnip's memory of her great horn thudding into something soft and heavy, and her head launching another weight into a wall. He had butchered his fair share of game and did not think, based on the sound the horn made as it stabbed into flesh, that the first man had survived, though the second might have. There was more yelling, and Elsyn's not inconsiderable weight flopped against Turnip's side. The other woman, the papery one, had vanished, as though she had not been there.

Here, at the last, was the thing that the cow wanted him to notice. A door had opened ahead and to their left, and based on the scent trail, the yelling man had vanished inside. An odd smell, like rotten wood and wisteria, whispered away through the door. It was not quite the same smell that the false Taryn had had about her, but close. It was a smell from underground and far away, of fairies who were constantly changing from one thing into another.

Abruptly they were out of the memory, and Turnip was showing him something else, another place she had smelled the weird fairy odor.

No, not another place; another person, someone who had come to the palace four weeks ago with his clothes reeking of it. It had dissipated after the first few days, allowing his natural smell to come through—

A smell that Kandar knew very well at this point.

"*Ben*," he said out loud. "Oh no."

PART FIVE

A cold, wet tongue in her ear woke Elsyn. She groaned and opened her eyes slowly, rubbing the crusty bits from her lashes. The brown nose of Onion's calf filled her vision, and she pushed him away. It was still very early, a few pale bars of sun glancing over the straw-covered floor.

Why did the dim blue light outside made her stomach pitch like a sinking ship?

The wedding. The wedding would happen today.

She clambered to her feet, evading the calf's questing mouth. He was hungry, and his mother was still dozing on the barn floor. Even in high summer, the stone building was chilly at this hour, and Elsyn wrapped her blanket tightly around herself.

The mattress she had borrowed from an empty dormitory room was rolled up and tucked onto a shelf between feed buckets. The calf's face was caressed and kissed, before she gave him a firm little shove toward where Onion was now chewing her cud, eyes closed. He scaled his mother's back and then fell off.

Elsyn wanted to walk to the cheesemaking room and start some soft rounds with last night's milk. Nothing too difficult, something she could do well even half-asleep. But if she did that, she might as well do the milking, and then she'd find something else that needed to be cleaned, something else that needed to be organized, and at the end of it she didn't think she'd be brave enough to go down to meet Kandar in the city temple. Dana, one of the few priests still staying in the palace temple, had already promised to see to the cows before the ceremony. Elsyn wouldn't use them as an excuse to avoid her other duties.

She found the short over-robe she'd hung up the night before on a metal hook, folded up the blanket, and forced her feet into a pair of canvas shoes.

The walk through the wet grass of the pasture cleared some of the tired fog filling her brain, as the heavy dew saturated her shift and stuck the fabric to her legs. Two the housekeepers had delivered and laid out her wedding garments the night before on the great bed in her parents' room: a robe of the finest, whitest, softest wool, that bore only a passing resemblance to the basic priest's shift; an under-robe of the finest linen; a heavy sash of of cloth-of-gold which her father had worn over his shoulders for religious ceremonies; finely made leather sandals.

It had taken her monumental willpower to enter that haunted room again, after a month of living entirely in the temple and the upper pastures. She still could not bring herself to sleep there.

There was an unpleasant gap between what a queen ought to do to prepare for her wedding and what a priest might do, even a theoretically high-ranking one. A queen ought to have attendants, women of rank chosen to show favor to their respective noble lineages. A priest ought to have companions, members of the same initiate class, typically drawn from merchant and farming families. The temple was extremely resistant to accepting noble children, as the political implications were always unpleasant. It had taken direct orders from the queen and prince-consort for Elsyn to be taken on.

The end result was that servants had cleaned the clothes she had requested, and she would get ready alone. She would be met by a group of priests and nobles in the throne-room, and they would accompany her down to the city's main temple, where Kandar and his retinue of goblins were waiting and the first of the rituals would be performed.

She wondered if the High Priest and Neddie would attend. Petra and the other priests still went vague and quiet when she asked about them, and after a while she had stopped asking rather than force them to betray any confidences.

The palace halls were unpleasantly silent, and she wondered how many of the staff had quietly given notice when their pay had stopped coming. Getting the royal accounts in order was another task she dreaded. The stewards viewed her with understandable hostility at this point. She wondered if Kandar knew anything about bookkeeping.

She wondered if Ben knew anything about bookkeeping.

As though her thought had summoned him, Ben rounded the corner of the hallway just ahead of her. He was dressed neatly in dark colors, a mail shirt glittering at the neck of his doublet and a cloak of deep red hanging from his shoulders. The sword belted at his waist did not look like a dress weapon. He had let his beard grow a little. He looked like a man, a great, dignified man.

He started, squaring his shoulders and visibly schooling his features to stillness before bowing. "Your Majesty—"

"Don't," she said, and she was too tired to keep the sadness out of her voice. *I shouldn't be the queen, and you shouldn't have been taken away from me.* "Please don't."

He opened his mouth and then pressed his lips together so tightly they went white.

"You are my honor guard," she said, after a long moment of breathing through her nose and focusing on a point over his right shoulder.

His ear dipped as he nodded silently.

"Very well. I have to wash and get dressed. It shouldn't take long." She turned down the next hall, nauseously aware of the pieces of straw still in her hair and the faded blanket clutched to her body.

Ben made as if to fall in behind her.

"No," she snapped. "Walk next to me."

When Ben saw Elsyn walking slowly down the hall toward him, her black hair luminous in the sun through the clerestories, her familiar face made new and wonderful by seven years, he loved her more than he had ever loved anyone.

He had shamed her, he had shamed himself, he had shamed his mother, and he did not want to be anywhere in the whole world except here.

"You can wait—" Elsyn looked around the entrance to her parents' chambers, feeling awkward. "Well, come inside the vestibule at least."

"Do you have a list of the approved attendants?" Ben asked, his voice careful and cool, a stranger's words in a familiar mouth. "I don't want to let anyone in who shouldn't be here."

"There aren't any attendants," she said. "I couldn't—it's only me."

"Then the servants," he said after a minute. "I'll have a list of who is helping you."

"I didn't see the point," she said, feeling her face get hot. "I can't have my hair dressed because of the crown and the horns have to fit over the top. There's no gown, just the robe. And I can't—I *won't* wear paint on my face. They can see what I look like."

He stared at her. He opened his mouth. He closed it.

"It will be fine," she said.

"Elsyn," he said, and that was his voice, Ben's voice, the voice she knew, "you have to be joking."

"I've been dressing myself without help for ten years," she shot back. She spun on her heel and marched through the vestibule, shouldering open the ancient oak door. It opened into a small receiving room. Her clothes were laid out in the bedroom beyond that.

Boot heels echoed against the flagstones, and she looked up from inspecting the ties on the beautiful leather sandals to see that Ben had followed her. His heavy eyebrows had drawn together to form a deep, worried wrinkle.

"Do you—" he started. His hands clenched, and he lifted his arms as though he would cross them over his chest, before slowly unfolding his fingers and laying them deliberately against his thighs. "Do you need help?" Silence dripped into the room, filling it to a suffocating level.

"Help," Elsyn repeated, feeling very stupid.

Ben took a step forward and met her eyes. "Your mother should be here with you," he said. "Or Taryn. They are not, and I am sorry. I am —I am a poor substitute for family, but perhaps better than nothing."

About a thousand times better than nothing, Elsyn almost said, but bit her lip. I wish I could have made Algenymmar understand. I wish I hadn't lost my temper, *again.*

"Very well," she said, wishing it didn't sound so wooden. She swallowed hard. "I know you can plait hair."

The memory that sentence elicited was so strong she squeezed her eyes shut. Ben had tried to teach her and Taryn to ride once, sneaking Pear, Quince's dam, into the palace through the priests' gate—and, she could only assume, with full cooperation of the priests. Pear had been even more patient than Quince, but nine-year-old Elsyn had spent most of the afternoon falling off. Taryn had gotten bored an hour into the proceedings and had vanished, reappearing some while later with a half-dozen hand pies she had stolen from the kitchens. Elsyn had been determined to learn, though, and had kept struggling back onto the saddle even after she'd bruised her knees, shins, and both shoulders.

What she remembered more sharply than any of the falls was Ben patiently taking down her hair at the end of the afternoon and combing out the bits of grass and moss and dirt with his fingers. He had braided her hair again and even made a brave attempt to pin it up the way Taryn's maid did.

"Elsyn?"

"I need to wash my hair," she said, opening her eyes. Before she could think better of it, she dropped her blanket on the table at the end of the bed and pulled her braid free from beneath her shift.

Ben eyed her as she unpicked the braid, which reached her waist in a thick coil. "Are you going to get married with wet hair?"

"I'm going to get married only smelling lightly of barn," she retorted, running her fingers over her scalp. "Kandar will be the only one close enough to smell the cows."

"I don't think Kandar minds," Ben said, and he was almost smiling.

That was too overwhelming to think about, and Elsyn hastily retreated to the alcove where the servants had left a full pitcher of water, a large basin, and a cake of milk soap. She rolled the soap through her hands and rubbed the lather over her skull and through the length of her hair. Sometime in the past she would have told Ben that the left side of her head was crunchy with cow slobber, but she couldn't imagine saying those words to this nobleman.

"If you sit, I can rinse for you," he said, close behind her.

After a moment, Elsyn nodded stiffly, and Ben pulled a chair away from the wall for her. She sat, feeling enormous and ungainly.

Ben's hands were much larger than she remembered. He took the heavy pitcher in one hand and cupped the back of her head in the other, tugging gently until she leaned back over the basin. Elsyn closed her eyes. A thin stream of cool water hit her hairline and ran down her skull. There was a soft tap as he set the pitcher down, and then smoothed the lather out of her hair, then poured again, then smoothed.

Elsyn's tight shoulders began to relax.

After what felt like a small eternity of his hand firmly supporting her skull, he coiled her hair and squeezed it over the basin. "There. Do you have a towel and comb?"

"In the drawer," Elsyn said, with difficulty.

The draw slid and clunked, and the objects inside rattled. Ben draped the towel around her neck and started combing the ends of her hair.

A wave of tingling moved over Elsyn's scalp and down her neck and back. *He's only doing this to be kind,* she thought, desperately calm. *It's nothing to do with me.*

Ben wrapped her hair in the towel and wrung it out again, then started to braid.

"Will your mother—" She stopped.

Ben paused in his braiding, his fingertips resting lightly on the nape of her neck. "Yes?"

All of the questions she wanted to ask seemed likely to have awful answers. *Is the Duke going to make a scene at the wedding? Have I made a mortal enemy? Has she tried to speak with you?*

"Does she still keep Pear in her stables?"

Ben continued braiding, then tied the end with a bit of leather and dropped it over her shoulder. "I don't know. I will have to ask her the next time we meet."

By noon, the sun blazed overhead, and the heat felt like it would crack the cobblestones.

Kandar had been waiting in the sanctuary of the city temple with Ildar since just before sunrise. Jolar had disappeared into the maze of narrow streets with half of the other goblins, searching for whatever premonition of malice was making all of their ears itch and their eyes water. Amlar and the rest were still at the palace. They and Ben would accompany Elsyn in her procession down the hill.

Kandar cursed his cousin for not giving him a more specific warning. Ildar could not tell him if something was being planned to disrupt the wedding, or if what they felt was no more than the concentrated hatred of a fairy-addled gentry. The wizard's ability to read the future was admittedly limited to meteorological occurrences and which horses would have trouble foaling. In any case, he stood by the great open door of the temple, a bow in his hand and a quiver and short-sword at his belt, tense and ready.

The city temple was in poor repair. The floor was missing dozens of tiles, and little piles of crumbled plaster from the ceiling dotted those that were left. Dozens of devotional niches to different gods lined the walls, but only eight were occupied, including the biggest pair for the Two-Bodied God at the front. They had only seen four priests, mostly very young or very old. The priests kept bringing out jugs of water and plates of stale biscuits for them.

From Elsyn, he understood that the first wedding rituals were witnessed by the general citizenry, as their monarchs were consecrated to the service of their subjects. Then they would process back up to the hill to the palace, where another set of rituals bound them to honor the memory of the royal ancestors.

Both ought to overseen by priests of the most senior rank, but the magnate of the city temple had died under distressingly questionable circumstances five years ago, and the High Priest of the palace temple was still refusing to communicate with them.

As he crouched before one of the empty devotional niches, Kandar thought about rituals, and Elsyn, and Ben. He wished they could go up into the mountains-just-to-the-left and light the wedding fires and run the ceremonial horse-races. He wanted his cousin the king to drink their health and offer them each a chalice filled with mare's milk. It took a very long time to call a shaman down from the farthest mountains, but he wanted to have the auguries read for the three of them and any children Elsyn might bear.

Time for that later, he told himself. They would get through today, and then it would be night-time, time for the last and most private ritual. There were apparently several prayers to be said and a special small cheese to be cut and eaten, before the marriage was consummated. He couldn't let himself think too much about the consummation or he would need to dunk himself in the public fountain.

He wondered if his ancestors would recognize Elsyn's prayers.

"They approach," Ildar said, from the doorway. "Prepare yourself."

Kandar jumped to his feet.

The two of them strode together to the door of the temple and out onto the colonnaded portico. The temple faced on a great square, and it already teemed with hundreds of onlookers. Most looked like craftspeople or farmers. A space close to the temple's entrance had been roped off for the noble families to watch the wedding in relative comfort, though very few were in attendance. A tall, dark-haired woman stood at the back of the temporary enclosure, wearing a long coat of Deragcaish red, accompanied by two retainers dressed in the same colors. Her lined features were an echo of Ben's. Kandar stared at her. Elsyn had said the Duke probably would not attend, without providing more details. Jolar had heard from Amlar who had heard from Hinat who had heard from Poll, a priest with a broken leg who had been living in Algenymmar's house for three weeks, that the queen had arrived with four of her splendid holy cattle to shout at the Duke for her conduct toward her son. Kandar wished very much he could have seen this.

Soldiers in yellow-trimmed palace doublets shouted and used their pole-arms to push their way through the plaza from the street opposite the temple entrance. Kandar couldn't yet see Elsyn. This plaza was separated from the main artery through the city by two smaller streets and a sharp corner. Motion flickered in the corner of his eye. Jolar and two other goblins both lay flat along the gutter of a building to his left. He saw other goblins at the back of the crowd, and one watching from an open window. That was Lendar, and he could just see the tip of her bow over the windowsill.

The royal procession turned the corner into the plaza. A line of white-robed priests, each wearing a giant set of metal horns, walked single file next to another line of richly-dressed nobles. Their progress toward the temple was excruciatingly slow, as citizens shouted and bowed to them and plucked at their sleeves.

A glint of true gold sparked at the back of the procession. Elsyn was another head taller than the other priests, and the horns she wore were taller still. As she passed, silence fell over the ranks of the city, and they became still. The hot air quivered.

Elsyn looked to neither her left nor her right. She walked through the crowd as she walked through the temple pastures, steady and full of purpose.

This must be what seeing a god is like, Kandar thought.

He dimly registered that a massive form that must be Ben paced very slowly at the end of the procession, behind Jolar and the other goblins. He hoped Ben could appreciate how magnificent Elsyn looked. He hoped—

That was the last clear thought he had before an arrow sprouted from Ben's chest, and pandemonium broke out.

Pain blossomed upward from Ben's collarbone. He looked down in disbelief at the green-fletched arrow suddenly lodged there. Where had *that* come from? His head shot up, triangulating the path of the missile. The archer must be shooting from the second floor of one of the buildings looking over the plaza. Ben yanked his sword free and was next to Elsyn in two long strides. Amlar and the goblins had already fanned out around the nobles and the priests, herding them into a tight ball behind their swords.

The crowd roared. Two children broke away from the sea of onlookers and sprinted away through the narrow street they had just marched down in stately slowness. Someone screamed very loudly and close by; another half-dozen people ran past.

Ben felt sick. He had never been in a riot, but the army captains had run drills on how to cut off a stampede every summer, and standing between a tight exit and a panicky crowd was maybe the most dangerous place he'd ever stood—

Black stars opened and spread across his vision. He shouldn't feel this ill. His hauberk was made of made of good steel; the arrow shouldn't have even gone through.

Ben stumbled and fell to his knees. Elsyn couldn't understand what she was seeing—the shouting of the terrified around her was so loud —had he tripped? What had he tripped on? Her mind could not make sense of the arrow in his chest. She turned to Amlar, who stood ahead of her, brandishing two swords. The goblin looked back at Ben, then at Elsyn, horror making her lips curl back over her tusks.

Amlar mouthed a word—or maybe she screamed it, because Elsyn could hear nothing, nothing at all, the cacophony of voices on all sides forming solid wall of sound that cut her off from everything.

Poison.

Elsyn look back down at Ben, and his face was white, tinged with green. She looked up at Amlar, flabbergasted, desperate for what was happening to not be happening, and the goblin said—screamed—howled another word—

Fairies.

The attack had come.

A fine network of thin blue lines laced themselves up Ben's neck and over his face. He gasped as though he were being choked by unseen hands. Slowly he toppled forward until he was lying in an ungainly heap on the pavement.

"You can't," Elsyn said out loud, "you'll be trampled," and now there were more and more people running past their goblin-guarded circle, pressing them in on each other, all sobbing, shouting, hysterical to escape. Part of her gibbered and wailed in chorus with the solid mass of terrified humanity on all sides.

What a gods-damned mess, a different part of Elsyn thought, though the words felt like they were coming to her from farther and farther away. Her body acted without her. She took off her horned crown and crouched in front of Ben, hauling him up against her chest until she could duck her head under his arm and stand up, most of his weight hanging from her shoulders. He was probably not heavier than a six-month-old calf.

"You have to walk," she said, and though surely he could not hear her, Ben was still conscious enough to feebly set one foot down in front of them other.

Someone—a priest?—set the crown back on her head—good, the crowd would able to see her and get out of the way.

Elsyn marched forward, her right hand clutching Ben's wrist, her left arm wrapped around his waist. He felt cold and clammy. She could feel herself shouting but could not hear the words.

The crowd parted again in front of her, and her eyes focused on a point ahead. The temple steps. They still seemed very far away. There was a tall figure standing up there, dressed in flame-bright clothes—

"Kandar," she shrieked, so loudly she thought the top of her skull might explode off. "Kandar, *help me*."

He leaped from the top of the steps, a jump that took him ten yards into the crowd, over the heads of dozens of shocked humans. Then he was running on all fours, a sort of ocean in animal form surging to meet her and Ben, until he was *there*, insinuating himself under Ben's other arm, and they could not run with his weight between them, but they marched double-time, and no one stood before them—

They came to the steps, and Elsyn counted. One. Two. Twenty. Thirty-four. They were at the top, and they both wheeled and faced out across the plaza. Elsyn could feel a great fear rising far away in whatever part of her could still think, a terror of what carnage might meet her eyes, but though the crowd had gone thin and frayed at the edges, there were no pools of blood or crushed bodies. The circle of goblins protecting the priests and nobles had been allowed to spread out again, and the goblins had let their weapons fall to half-readiness. Soldiers in the palace livery had reappeared at the edges of the plaza, looking somewhat the worse for wear, their uniforms torn and several of them missing helmets. More goblins had materialized from somewhere to join them at the perimeter, shouting that they had found the archers—*archers?*—and the good cityfolk could calm themselves.

The enclosure for the nobles to watch the wedding had been broken apart and crushed into splinters on the pavement. Elsyn saw none of the nobles she knew were supposed to be there, with one vivid exception. Algenymmar and her retainers had herded a small group of citizens up the stairs to shelter on the temple portico and were now standing guard in front of them. The duke had drawn her sword, and her servants both held long staffs. Behind them, a dozen very old, very young, and injured individuals stood on the pediment, fear written over their faces.

Elsyn thought of Bean, and how the Boss Cow's mind-voice sounded. Usually it was a bellow, just below the range of human hearing. Just once, when Bean had faced the false Taryn and struck a horn into her heart, Elsyn had heard her voice ring through the stones of the palace walls with the resonance of the god-favored.

I am boss cow, she thought, and this is my herd. Two-Bodied God, let them hear me!

"I AM YOUR QUEEN," she said, and the words rolled away from her like thunder rippling over the plains after a lightning strike. "I WILL KEEP YOU AND GUARD YOU, MY PEOPLE, WHO ARE BELOVED OF THE GODS."

The reverberations of her voice trembled through the flagstones of the plaza. Several people fell down, but no one ran away. Instead, Elsyn felt hundreds of pairs of eyes fix on her.

Well, probably on her gleaming horns, but that was good enough.

She half-turned, not daring to let Ben sag, and spoke again. "KANDAR, SON OF USDAR," and whatever magic was in her now unfortunately did not allow her to remember any more of his lineage, "DO YOU ACCEPT THE STEWARDSHIP OF THE PEOPLE WHO ARE BELOVED BY THE GODS?"

She couldn't turn enough to see his face, but she felt him move his arm to better grip the limp body between them. She didn't know if he understood about Bean's god-voice or if he was just caught in the edge of this magic, but his baritone was loud enough to shake the roof-tiles. "I ACCEPT THEIR STEWARDSHIP, AND I SHALL HUMBLY SERVE THEIR QUEEN."

"THEN I TAKE YOU AS MY HUSBAND AND CONSORT," Elsyn said, and whatever parts of the ritual they had skipped—the formulas which had not been spoken, the high-ranking witnesses they didn't have, the libations which had not been poured—apparently didn't matter to the Two-Bodied God, because she felt the oath-magic snap into place with those words. A great force pulled her down, into the earth, and out, toward all the people watching her, and then toward Kandar, almost smashing Ben's body as the same energy yanked him toward her, before the power let go and she could stand upright again.

Elsyn gasped and wavered on her feet. She felt like she might vomit.

"Help," she said, but Ildar was there suddenly with two other goblins she didn't know, and they were taking Ben between them and carrying him into the dark door of the temple.

"So you didn't catch the archers?" Kandar hissed at Jolar.

They marched behind Ben's litter, though that was a fancy word for two cloaks stretched between six goblins. Ildar had removed his doublet and hauberk and found the fairy arrowhead where it had lodged under his collarbone. He pried the malevolent little dart loose with a small silver penknife. When it fell to the floor he spat and cursed at it in a language no one else knew, and it burst into blue flame. As soon as the wizard blew the ash away, the blue net of sickly lines faded from Ben's skin. His horribly white, rigid face relaxed, and he drew a deep breath. He had still not awakened, but Kandar had rested an ear against his chest, and his inhalations were steady and even.

"No," Jolar hissed back. "I'm not even sure if there was more than one, or if the other arrows shot into the crowd were glamours. We didn't find any arrowheads."

Algenymmar—Ben's mother! what a terrifying woman!—had tried to insist that her son be taken back to her house, but Elsyn only stared at her blankly. After a few minutes of silence between the two great women, the duke bowed, her lips pressed together in a thin line, and left the temple.

Kandar, who only an hour before had been thinking very nasty thoughts about Algenymmar, did not know what to make of her now. From the temple steps he had watched the duke assess the impending stampede and then dive into the crowd to grab the closest cityfolk near her who could not keep up with a running crowd, dragging them up onto the steps and out of the way of the crush. The other nobles had vanished like smoke when the panic had started.

The procession now consisted of only five priests, two nobles, and thirty goblins. Elsyn walked at the front, her shoulders very straight and her chin very high under the golden horns.

Her neck must be exhausted, Kandar thought, and in spite of the horror packed into the last hour, his pulse quickened at the thought of her taking off the crown and lying down to rest.

The ritual of consecration to the honor of the royal family was performed in the throne room. Elsyn did not feel any great and ancient magic take hold of her body when she spoke the memorized words to the bedraggled group left to hear them, and Kandar's voice did not boom through the building like an avalanche when he recited his part.

Ben lay on the floor behind them, the cloaks wrapped over his broad chest, his head tipped to one side, his cheek resting on the stone floor. She had touched her fingers to his lips to make sure she felt air moving before they had begun.

"We witness the union of queen and prince consort," said one of the priests, and the other priests repeated it, then the nobles, then the goblins. "May they be known by the ancestors." The priest bowed to each other and bowed to the nobles and then bowed to her, presenting her with a small round package wrapped in brown paper. The holy cheese.

Then the priests and the nobles were filing away, disappearing into the hall that led out into the temple pastures above the palace, leaving Elsyn and Kandar facing each other, surrounded by goblins.

He suddenly shook his head vigorously, making his ears bend and flap against his face, before looking at her, one eyebrow raised. "Are you all right?"

"No," she said, surprised into the truth. "I mean—" She rubbed her eyes with one hand, clutching the cheese of consummation in the other. "Let's just get this over with," she whispered.

Jolar stepped forward. "Ben can stay with us until he wakes up," she said, nodding to the body on the floor.

"*No,*" Elsyn said, at the same time as Kandar said, "NO." She couldn't look at him just now to see what his face was doing. She rushed on, "He stays with me—with us. I don't want—I'm afraid—he won't notice anything. He's asleep." She took a deep breath. "I don't want to let him out of my sight, just now."

"What if he wakes up?" Ildar asked, his voice dry. "While you are —?"

"Is he likely to wake up?" Elsyn asked in a brittle voice.

Ildar was quiet, then said, "I do not think so, not for three or four days. The poison used on that arrow was a strong one, and it will take a long time for his body to sweat it out."

"Then please help me—please help us carry him to the royal chambers." I need to be able to protect him, she almost said, but that sounded completely mad, so she bit her lip and remained silent.

Jolar jerked her head at Ildar, and he bowed to her. The six goblins who had carried Ben up the hill gripped the edges of the cloaks again and followed Elsyn down the hall.

After a brief perusal of the options in the royal bedchamber, they laid Ben in the bed, before filing out the door. She thought she heard each of them mutter something short to Kandar, a blessing maybe, as they passed by him.

"We'll make do," Elsyn said to Jolar's raised eyebrows. "This shouldn't take long." The goblin captain gave her a salute, perhaps ironic, and left.

And now the door was closed, and she was alone with Kandar and the unconscious Ben.

Elsyn took off her horned crown and her golden sash and set them on a table against the wall of the room. She suddenly looked very tired, dark smudges visible under each eye.

She picked up the cheese again and turned to him, offering the small package. "I don't think I can remember the words," she said. "But we ought to eat—I mean—it's traditional—"

Kandar considered her large brown hands, how they folded neatly around the cheese. He wanted—no, he was not going to get ahead of himself.

Instead, he stepped onto the bed with a motion like a stork hopping through a river, drawing up his other leg in a crouch. Ben's weight shifted, and he mumbled. "Come sit," Kandar said, tapping the coverlet beside him.

"I thought—" She took a step toward him, then stopped. "We had better get it over with." She wouldn't meet his eyes.

"Regardless of the speed at which the act is performed, you are going to have to be a bit closer than a yard away," Kandar said. "Come sit, and we will eat the magic cheese."

"It's not magic," Elsyn said, but she finally complied, gingerly sinking down onto the mattress next to him. The extra weight was enough to make Ben's body shift. Carefully she unfolded the brown paper, revealing a fresh white round that sat in the hollow of her palm, a sprig of herbs pressed into the top. "It's mixed milk," she explained, breaking the round in half and passing him one piece. "Cow, sheep, and goat. It's supposed to represent the bounty of the kingdom."

Kandar sniffed the cheese. The tiny dried flowers on the top emitted a spicy, unfamiliar scent. He took a bite. It was very good cheese, nutty and tangy and buttery. He popped the second bite into his mouth and looked at Elsyn out of the corner of his eye. She was still holding the cheese, staring down at it as though she wasn't sure what to do.

He did not think, as he often did not think in this sort of situation, and he reached over to lightly touch her palm. She startled, looking up at him. They were shoulder to shoulder now, and their faces were very close. Kandar took the piece of cheese out of her hand and held it to her lips.

Elsyn stared at him. It was true that he was generally distracted by her shoulders or her legs or her hands when he was near her, but she did have very beautiful large, dark eyes.

She took a deep breath through her nose and tentatively opened her mouth, taking the cheese from his fingers and chewing slowly.

Kandar watched her throat as she swallowed.

"We should," she started. "Um. Well." Ben emitted a sound like a little snore, and they both looked back at him, but his eyes were shut tight.

"How much do you know about this?" Kandar asked.

"Enough," Elsyn said, sounding defensive. "I've seen cows put with the bull. And I've overheard—sometimes the other priest initiates— when a lot of teenagers are in a dormitory together—"

"Right," Kandar said, rearranging his notions. He had somehow assumed—Elsyn was the most attractive human he'd ever encountered, barring Ben—he glanced anxiously behind him, but Ben's chest was rising and falling normally. He hadn't imagined that she'd had a parade of lovers —the false Taryn surely would have used that against her—but he had thought there had been someone.

He had wondered if she and Ben had ever been together, but that thought seemed best to keep to himself.

"The bull might have given you the wrong idea," he said finally. "With, er, non-seasonal beasts, it takes longer for everyone involved—"

Elsyn flushed a little under her tan. Kandar's brain chose that moment to desert him entirely, and he leaned forward and nipped her ear.

Kandar leaned forward and nipped her ear. Part of Elsyn, a small, scared, hurt part, wanted to shove him away. You don't need to pretend to like me, that part wanted to shout. You don't have to pretend you want go to bed with a giant cow of a woman. You want to be prince-consort and I need your help. That's enough. We don't have to playact like we're in love.

Her shoulders ached from half-carrying Ben across the temple plaza—she glanced back at him; he looked fine—her throat burned from speaking with the voice of a god, and her legs hurt from marching up and down stone streets.

A very, very small part of her, the part of her with the taste of the buttery ritual cheese still in her mouth, wanted to nip Kandar back and see what happened.

She struggled for a long moment and said, "I appreciate your kindness. It is awkward for me."

"Yes, we should have practiced this a few dozen times," he said.

Her face felt very hot. She reached for the buttons at the neck of his wedding shirt and unhooked them, because that seemed helpful and like it would need to happen at some point. Kandar let out a short bark of laughter and shrugged out of his scarlet vest, then tugged the orange shirt over his head. He draped both over the headboard and looked back at her, a little challenging.

The musculature of his body was not proportioned quite the same way as a human's, and the fine, dark fur over his face, neck, and hands also grew over the rest of his body. Before she could think better of it, Elsyn stroked his collarbone. The fur was smooth and stiff, like the guard hairs of a cow's pelt. She didn't think he would appreciate the bovine comparison, but he was very pleasant to touch.

"Now you," he said.

"Now me what?" she said, and then realized what he meant. "No."

"How do you think this is going to work if you're still clothed?" he asked.

The truth was that she had refused to think about it, because the thought of taking her clothes off in front of another person made her feel sick. "Under the blanket," Elsyn said finally.

"It's midsummer," Kandar said, cocking his head to one side. His face was still very close to hers. He put his hand on her waist. "I would like to see you."

Elsyn tried to think, but her brain fizzed and popped like peas thrown into hot oil. Probably she should take off her outer robe, in any case; it was too nice a garment to get wrinkled. She stood and tugged at the shoulders, pulling it over her head as Kandar had done.

The fine linen under-robe provided less protection that she had hoped; it was damp with her sweat and partially transparent in places. For a moment she got stuck looking down at her self, staring at her heavy belly and massive thighs. Her breasts were … some of the cruelest comments made by the false Taryn's lackeys had been about that part of her body and how much like a cow they made her.

There was just such a *lot* of her. Her face burned.

She just needed to get through this. "How do you need me to—to be, so you can do what needs done?" she asked, not looking at Kandar.

He was a quiet for a moment, and then he said, "Sit up at the head of the bed, with your legs in front of you."

Elsyn climbed back on the bed. In spite of herself, she tried to work out the geometry of what they were going to do, since Kandar clearly wasn't going to go at it like a bull would. She sat just in front of the bolster at the head of the bed. Ben's face, his jaw slack in sleep, was on a level with her hip.

She should have been embarrassed to have him there, but at the moment she could not muster any emotion other than relief that he was still breathing regularly.

"So I—uh—I lie back?" she said, wondering why Kandar thought it would be comfortable to rest on the oaken headboard. There were a lot of holly leaves carved in high relief to gouge one's back with their sharp tips.

"No, stay there," he said. He crawled toward her, his orange eyes very bright, his crest standing up very straight. "Now pull your knees up to your chest."

That seemed counterproductive, but Elsyn did it.

Kandar brought his face close to hers again. He didn't kiss her—

kissing was clumsy for goblins, because of the tusks—but he nuzzled her chin and then her neck. It felt very nice, and Elsyn briefly wished the gods would accept neck-nuzzles as consummation, and that she could get pregnant with a royal heir from them.

Now he moved his face lower and pressed it between her collarbones. That was also nice, and absently she stroked the fingers of both hands along the sides of his crest and down the back of his skull.

For a minute, Kandar breathed hard against her chest.

Curiously, he did not then lift himself to get into a position where he could get on top of her, but dipped his head lower, until his face was squished between her breasts. That should have been horrifying, and Elsyn wanted to tell him to stop because he ought to be ignoring that part of her body, but also he was nibbling on her through the thin shift and she very much did not want him to stop doing that.

Her knees had unconsciously fallen open to accommodate the width of Kandar's upper body as he pressed his face against her chest. He was not fat like her, but he was still a very large person by human standards, and his weight and solidity was reassuring.

What was also unexpectedly nice were his large ears pressed against the sensitive skin between her breasts. He twitched them constantly in a way that was hard to see but easy to feel. She touched the tips lightly, before drawing her fingers down the backs of his ears, against the grain of his fur, until her hands rested the muscles of his neck, which were also quivering. Elsyn wondered wistfully if married people who didn't need to prove themselves to the gods and the country at large did this sort of thing all the time.

The under-robe caught on her knees, making it impossible to relax further, and impatiently she twitched the hem up to her hip. Kandar made an odd noise and pushed his face into her belly. She definitely did not want him to do that, or to use his teeth and pointed tongue to explore the rolls that formed above and below her navel—probably she should stop petting the back of his head and tell him to stop that—

Abruptly he pushed his face between her legs, and Elsyn could not think about anything else.

She knew what the other young priests had been doing when they crept into each other's bunks in the dormitory, sticking their hands up each other's robes. It had not occurred to her that someone could use his mouth for a similar purpose, but now it did, forcefully. As a teenager, Elsyn, awakening in the early morning darkness from a particular kind of dream, had touched herself between her legs in utter silence, stopping if she heard a grunt or snore from another bed. It had been an unsatisfying experience, and the threat of embarrassment had loomed so large that she had stopped altogether after a few years.

Kandar's mouth was warm and his tongue was rough. He quickly nosed between her folds and found the tender nub at the top. After a few minutes she found herself moving her hips against his face, trying to heighten the sensation. Her whole body throbbed with the beat of her heart. She clenched her jaw, trying not to make a sound, and her legs trembled.

Part of her howled. This isn't how people got pregnant! This isn't anything! What is he *doing!*

She told that part of her to shut up.

There were people talking quietly nearby. The right side of Ben's chest ached, from the top of his shoulder down to the bottom of his rib cage, but he was otherwise comfortable, lying on something soft. His mail was gone, as were his boots. There were good, familiar smells here; a faint tang of cheese, the earthy, grassy smell of goblin, and a human smell that he recognized but couldn't name.

A snort and some laughter came from above him. The surface he was lying on shifted, as though a weight had come to rest by his head. His eyelids felt as heavy as stones, and he couldn't make out the words being said, only that there were two different voices.

Ben couldn't remember why he hurt or why he was lying down, but it seemed like neither of those things ought to be true. There was somewhere important he needed to be, something important he needed to do. He did not especially want to get up, but he should find out if he were shirking his duty, whatever that may be.

Another weight pulled the surface he was resting on to one side, enough so that he slid and bumped into something warm—a leg? The sources of the voices were very close indeed. It felt like he had a heavy black blanket draped over his head, numbing all his senses. It was only with considerable effort that he forced himself to feel each of the fingers in his right hand, feel them and then slowly bend each one. Yes. He was waking up. The voices were a little more distinct, though they didn't seem to speaking now, only breathing heavily.

He could feel his right elbow and now his shoulder. He stretched out a hand to touch whoever was next to him, to let them know he was awake and ask for their help figuring out what he was supposed to be doing right now. His fingertips found smooth skin. He brushed it lightly, then stretched his hand wide and lightly squeezed whichever limb he had found.

The heavy breathing stuttered and then stopped. A hand covered his and pressed it firmly against that smooth skin, and a familiar voice asked, "Ben? Ben, are you awake? All you all right?"

Those syllables cut the rest of the way through his strange torpor, and he inhaled sharply and opened his eyes, still clutching at the person next to him.

It took him a long minute to understand what he was seeing. Elsyn sat on the bed next to him, her black hair in disarray, her face quite red. She was wearing a garment like her usual shift but much thinner; he could clearly see the outlines of her body in the last sunlight through the arrowslit window over the bed. His hand had found the top of her thigh, and her hand pressed his tight to her bare leg. After a moment he realized her shift was pushed up around her waist. From his vantage point lying down, he could just see the dark-furred tip of a pointed ear over the curve of her leg.

The ear emerged fully as Kandar lifted his head. His eyes sparkled as they met Ben's, and he made a soft *harumph*ing sound that happy goblins often exchanged. "I am well-pleased to see you back among the living," he said. "Ildar said you might not wake for three days, the poison on the arrow was so strong."

"May the God be among us, I was worried about you—" Elsyn said, a note of panic creeping into her voice on the last word. Her other hand scrabbled among the bedlinens until she flopped the coverlet over her lap. "I am sorry. I had thought you wouldn't wake—and I was scared to leave you alone—and I thought this would be over—*quickly*—" There was a note of accusation in the last word, and Kandar snorted loudly.

"That's not my fault. You're as tense as a ten-string fiddle. I don't think I'd even fit in you as yet."

Ben found, to his horror, that feeling had returned to other parts of his body besides his left arm. With a monumental effort, he rolled away from Elsyn, pulling his hand off her leg, until he was face-down on the royal bed and she could not see how he was reacting to seeing her stripped to the waist and hearing Kandar talk about what they would soon be doing together. Blood suffused his cheeks until he felt sure he was as red as a boiled crab. It was one thing to realize his love for a beloved childhood friend at a remove, like a god's devotee; it was quite another, disgusting thing to be sick with envy of Kandar, her husband, for enjoying her large, beautiful, physical body—

Ben sucked in a deep breath and lifted his head. "Did the wedding —did the wedding go off? Were you able to do the rituals?"

"All but the last," Kandar said, his voice very dry. "Though we did eat the ceremonial cheese, so perhaps the gods will recognize it."

"I'll go in the next room," Ben said.

"We'll go in the next room," Elsyn said immediately. "You shouldn't get up yet—"

"I can get up—"

"I'm sure we can manage—"

"I am very tired and do not wish to fuck on the floor of a closet," Kandar said. There was a sound of fabric moving across fabric, and when Ben looked to the foot of the bed the goblin had curled into a large, offended lump, his back to both of them. One ear twitched.

His words cut through some barrier that had been keeping exhaustion at bay. Elsyn slid down in the bed until she was lying next to Ben. It was almost more than he could bear not to reach out and touch her arm.

"We will try again tomorrow," he heard her whisper into the gathering shadows.

Elsyn woke in darkness. She lay still for a long moment before she realized what had jarred her from sleep: She was breath-takingly, overwhelmingly *hot*. The heavy stone walls of the palace absorbed the heat of even the sixteen hours of daylight on the summer solstice, but she felt as though she were sleeping between two furnaces.

… or a very large man and a very large goblin.

Suddenly the royal chamber felt like it was getting smaller and tighter by the second.

She slid off the edge of the bed and padded to the wardrobe where her shifts were hung. Her fine linen under-robe was sticky and crunchy in places, and she was glad she couldn't see the stains left on it by yesterday's activities. After a moment of thought, Elsyn hung it from the door of the wardrobe. She hoped the servants would assume the correct thing, whatever that may be.

For a moment she stood quite naked in the darkness. The stone was cold under her feet, and the air was cool away from the bed.

Did Ben have a fever? she wondered. It seemed early for infection to set in, but she didn't know what effect fairy poison might have.

Her searching fingers found a long kirtle in the wardrobe, and she self-consciously laced it on before dropping a fresh shift over her head. Her whole body felt tender and vulnerable, and the extra clothing offered an added layer of protection.

She had not been allowed to study most of the veterinary training that the temple offered—at first because it was shocking that a princess would be taught such things as examining excrement for parasites and lancing infected wounds, and later because the veterinary priests had vanished along with the rest. Her medical knowledge was limited to first aid and superstition, but at this moment, after she had felt a god speaking through her body, she thought the superstition was worth a try.

She followed the hallways out through the throne room and into the pasture. The breeze felt like a drink of cold water, and stars stretched away across the unclouded sky. Elsyn hugged herself and set out across the grass. It had barely been a full day, and everything was already so different.

She accidentally woke Bean when she tripped on an unseen hoof.

HAVE BULLS NOW? the cow asked sleepily.

Elsyn felt her face go a little red. "I am married, yes."

CAREFUL WITH BULLS, Bean warned. GET IDEAS. The last word was barely distinguishable from dream-noises, and when Elsyn touched her neck the cow had already fallen back asleep.

The cheese she wanted was very rarely made. It relied on having sufficient moonlight in early spring to do a third milking after the cows had been on pasture where a certain wildflower grew abundantly. The cheese was made outdoors, also in moonlight, and aged for three to five years. Its peculiar properties came from a confluence of the Two-Bodied God, the Moon Cow, and the prickly deity of the wildflower.

If the false Taryn had known of it, she surely would have banned the priests from making it or storing it, as the cheese was said to break spells, disperse illusions, and unknot curses.

Elsyn went into the cheese-aging room, lit the lamp hanging from the wall, swept the floor with a broom, and then used a skewer to clear the dirt crusted around the trapdoor set in the back corner. It didn't look like anyone had been down to check on the special cheeses for a long time, which didn't bode well for anything being left below.

The cellar below was so small she had to duck her head to move past the staircase, and she almost knocked the lamp hanging from the ceiling to the floor. She had only been down here a handful of times. The wooden shelves were mostly bare, and several had collapsed. At the very back were three great rounds sitting defiantly on a middle shelf. She wondered when they had been brought down.

Elsyn squinted at the top shelf in the flickering light. There was an odd shadow at the back of it, and when she reached her hand through the dust, she found that a deeper recess had been carved into the stone of the wall behind. A stone box would keep a delicate cheese cooler than an open shelf.

Her fingers encountered something smooth and hard; a cheese-aging tray carved from wood. She drew it out, and yes, here was a single cheese, as wide as her forearm was long and about a palm in height. It was wrapped in birch bark, and a moon was pressed into the top.

Elsyn was so delighted with her find that she almost knocked Neddie down when she emerged from the trapdoor into the cheese-aging room. The accountant was standing between two racks of shelves, facing the door and wringing her hands. When the cheese tray bumped into her back, she whirled and started to babble before Elsyn could utter a word of apology.

"Oh, there *is* someone here—thank the gods—I have to find— have you seen—oh, *Your Majesty*," she sputtered. Her eyes were very big and her pale hair stuck straight out from her scalp, giving her the overall appearance of terrified scarecrow. "I—well—I did need to talk—oh, the God in Their Bodies! This is all a mess."

Elsyn was glad her hands were occupied with the cheese board, because otherwise she might have grabbed Neddie and shaken her. "Where have you been?" she hissed. "I haven't seen you in a month!"

"I wasn't—I was told not to—"

"Told by *whom?*" Elsyn demanded. "Who has authority over your queen? Who are you obligated to before *your queen?*" I know it's Algenymmar and the High Priest, but I want to know *why!* she thought furiously.

"It's not so much a matter of authority," Neddie said weakly, backing up a step. "We are bound first to the temple and the service of the God, and if supporting one claimant or another if the best way to serve them—"

"What other claimant is there?" Elsyn asked, so angry she could barely spit the words out. "Who is *we?* I am a priest. I have opened the priest-door. I care for the cows. I make cheese. I am helping Petra distribute the cheese. What other *we* is there, that somehow does not include me?"

"Historically, I mean," Neddie went on hastily. "Oh, I'm making a hash of this. What I meant to say is that we—I—that is—"

"I've heard enough," Elsyn said, moving to push past the accountant.

"There were *portents!*" the accountant said, sounding close to tears. "Usually the Two-Bodied God doesn't care one way or another who's on the throne—it's not really their specialty—but there were *portents* confirming the marriage yesterday, all through the city. I can't—it doesn't matter what she says, I can't go against the God. I can't be expected to go against the God!"

"Who is *she?*" Elsyn asked. Neddie licked her lips, and Elsyn could see she was getting ready to lie. "Algenymmar," she said, and Neddie's flinch was confirmation enough. "She's kept you from meeting with me for six weeks, or even acknowledging the wedding. What did she think she was going to accomplish?"

"I don't think she believed you were free of fairy influence," Neddie said weakly. "There was talk of bringing in a cousin—" Elsyn snarled.

"—but I don't think they can do that now!" Neddie rushed on. "Not now that you and the goblin prince clearly have the favor of the God! Maybe gods, plural! It's very hard to tell with these things."

"Right, so you've decided to throw your lot in with me now that the alternative looks too dangerous," Elsyn said sarcastically. "Does the High Priest know you are here? I suppose they do not dare disagree with Algenymmar, or leave the safety of her house?"

"Neither of them know that I am here," Neddie said. "I believed they were doing the right thing to seek stability for the kingdom, but now I know that they are not. I was hoping to talk to you and explain."

Elsyn was silent, trying to stem the flood of anger clawing its way up her throat.

"Now that it is clear that you are *not* a fairy puppet, and have an official liaison with the goblin kingdom, it would perhaps be a good time to negotiate with the Duke for further support," Neddie said hopefully. This was clearly was she had wanted to say from the start, and her entire body deflated a little once she had delivered these words. "I know you have had some differences of late—"

"I stood on her stairs and screamed at her that she was a

dishonorable coward for abandoning her son," Elsyn said. She waited a moment to see if that statement embarrassed her; no, it did not. "Somehow I doubt she is at all eager to speak with me."

"Very large differences!" Neddie said. "But I believe—I'm sure we can get her to see reason now. I will argue for you. The High Priest values my opinion, and Algenymmar—well—Algenymmar listens closely to them. Please trust me."

"Of all the—you led me into an *attack*," Elsyn snapped. "I got *bashed in the head*. If Turnip hadn't followed me into the city, I might have *died*. Why on earth do you deserve my trust at this point?"

"That—that was a mistake," Neddie said weakly.

"A mistake?" Elsyn repeated. "A *mistake?*"

"I may have misrepresented the situation somewhat," she said, not meeting Elsyn's eyes. "At that time, it had seemed like it might be best if you became—a—a guest in the duke's house, until we could get things sorted out."

"I suppose it would have suited her if she had control of the queen," Elsyn said. Her stomach hurt with rage. It was one thing to suspect that someone she had known her whole life as a distant but basically trustworthy aunt had turned on her; it was another to have it confirmed that Algenymmar saw her as a large, awful doll that could be stuffed in a box when she wasn't needed. "Though it might have been inconvenient for her if one of her men had accidentally killed the queen."

"That shouldn't have happened. That wasn't her order at all. I don't know how her men could have misunderstood. They have been— the whole house has been very strange, of late."

"Good night, Neddie," Elsyn said.

"The situation has changed," Neddie went on, her voice pleading. "She is—she has been the temple's best ally, through all the horrors of the last years. Please, you must speak with her."

"I will consider it," Elsyn said, suddenly tired. "Good night, Neddie."

"I have some cheese for you," said a voice very close to Ben's ear.

He blinked blearily. His head ached, and the pain in his collarbone had returned with interest.

There was a faint light somewhere off to his left, but directly

147

above him was Elsyn's face. Her dark braid hung over one shoulder and coiled over his arm. He wanted to ask her to let him plait it smoothly again, but aside from the fact that he wasn't sure whether his right hand would cooperate, he didn't think he could pretend that he only wanted to touch her with the kindness of an old friend.

She looked down at him steadily for a long moment, before sitting back on the coverlet. Kandar, disturbed by the movement, stretched and yawned, his back briefly an elegant curve much longer than the bed. He folded in on himself again, regarding them both with lamplight glinting in his eyes. "Are we trying again, then?"

"I don't want Ben to move just yet."

"He doesn't have to move. He can help."

Ben stared at the underside of the bed's canopy and thought about cold things: snow, frozen rivers, mountaintops, wind through a tent in the dead of night …

"That's not—look here," Elsyn said, her cheeks darkening. She produced an improbably large cheese wrapped in thin strips of bark from a fold of her shift. "Ben should eat some of this. We have other things we need to talk about right now. I have just received some—some disturbing news."

The cheese, when unwrapped, unleashed a wave of acerbic stench akin to unwashed feet. Ben wrinkled his nose but allowed Elsyn to place a slice in his mouth. The curd was very smooth and a little sweet. He chewed thoughtfully.

"I want some," Kandar said from over Elsyn's shoulder. She cut another piece and he took it from her hand with his teeth.

"Ben," she said, once he had swallowed, "this is about your mother."

His shoulders tensed, and a lance of pain speared downward from the arrow wound.

Elsyn took a deep breath, fiddling with the penknife she had used to cut the cheese. "The high priest of the palace disappeared two years ago. I had thought—the remaining priests had assumed they were dead. Shortly after you left to find Ben—" here she glanced at Kandar "—I was able to find them by way of the temple accountant, Neddie. She'd never left, and no one noticed her. I thought—well, I didn't have any better ideas about how to get in touch with the other priests, and didn't know Petra was working in the city." Her tone when she said this last sentence was defensive, as though one of them would tell her she was an idiot for how she'd gone about things.

She stopped, looking uncertain, and cut another piece of cheese, which she offered to Ben. He took it, thinking. Kandar's eyes were narrowed, and he stared into the darkness outside the bed curtains.

"It seems foolish enough now, but Neddie told me she'd arranged a meeting with the high priest and Algenymmar, and I thought it was a step in the right direction. Only on the night I went with her to meet the duke, I was attacked before we ever reached the house."

Ben stopped chewing and sat up. His right arm was tingling all over, but he couldn't focus on that now. "*Wha—*" He heard the outrage in his own voice and quickly modulated his tone. "*What?* You were *attacked?* You don't mean—"

"Turnip told me," Kandar said. "But you should have said something earlier."

"I was embarrassed," Elsyn said. "And I wasn't sure the duke arranged it. It could have been random."

"What?" said Ben.

"Lie back *down,* until I know if the cheese worked," Elsyn said forcefully.

Ben complied, then repeated, "*What?*"

"Turnip is one of the herd," she said.

Ben almost sat up again, until he registered the two sets of glaring eyes aimed at him. "Please explain a little more," he said finally. "I'm injured and I can't think straight. Why are you talking about the cows?"

"Turnip followed me to the meeting I was supposed to have with your mother, and when I was attacked she—well—never mind what she did, but she got me back to the palace. I wasn't sure who was behind the attack then, or if anyone was. We weren't anywhere near the Deragcaish house, we were just going up the Street of the Bursars on the far side of the hill—"

"The servants' entrance," Ben said, feeling ill. His chest and arm were now burning all over. "There's a tunnel that cuts through the rock from the cellars and comes out on the Street of the Bursars. They must have come out there."

Elsyn's breath caught. "Then that—yes, that matches up with what Neddie said."

Now it was Kandar's turn to frown. He bumped Elsyn's shoulder with his face, like a large cat. "When did you talk to this Neddie? She doesn't sound any too trustworthy."

"I didn't seek her out," Elsyn said. "She found me in the cheese-aging room just now. The High Priest has been hiding in Algenymmar's house, and since the night of the attack Neddie's been hiding there too. She said she had come tonight without them knowing, because the God sent portents that convinced her during the wedding. She said the attack was a *misunderstanding*."

The last word rolled over Ben like a blow, and if he hadn't been already lying down, he might have stumbled. He had left his home seven years ago because he had shamed his family so deeply that he couldn't stand to look into his mother's disappointed, rage-filled face for a single more minute. He knew what he had done and what he had not done, but he had been so sure in every fiber of his being that banishment was fit sentence for the dishonor he had brought to her, who he respected above all people, whose goodwill he desired above all things.

And she had paid him back by hurting his queen, his friend, *Elsyn*. Not honestly, not directly, but under cover of darkness, where no one could be sure that Algenymmar was to blame.

Gods, he was *furious*.

"There is another thing you should know," Kandar said, and his gravelly voice cut through the cloud of anger filling Ben's skull. "Another thing Turnip told me about the attack."

"I have to talk to her," Ben said.

"Turnip smelled fairy magic in the servants' passage that the attackers came out of," the goblin said. "And she smelled it on *you*, Ben, when you'd just come back from the ducal house."

Ben sat up again and stared at Kandar. Elsyn turned and did the same.

"Why didn't you say that before?" she demanded.

"When?" Kandar asked, very reasonably. "Turnip only cornered me last night. You'd better ask her why she didn't tell anyone sooner."

"Cows don't have the best sense of time," Elsyn said.

"I have to talk to my mother," Ben repeated. He stretched his right arm; the burning had subsided, and now it felt almost normal. "I have to—this has gone on long enough."

"Ben," Elsyn said. He looked up at her and saw that her face had gone pale. "Do you remember the cluster of weird fairy events on Petra's map?" she asked quietly. "You said that a lot of them were close to Iuliud Glascrann's house, next to your mother's."

"So the open fairy door you've been looking for—" Ben rubbed his face. "Has probably been in my mother's house all along."

"Look on the bright side," Kandar said. "That might not be the only one."

PART SIX

The servants' tunnel was cold and very dark. The lantern hooks had been left to hang empty, and the camouflaged door from the street fit so tightly against the stones on either side that not a splinter of daylight could enter once it was closed.

Kandar did not need the light. His forefathers had spent entire centuries below the earth.

More importantly, the smell of fairy magic in this corridor was so strong that a human child could have followed it. Foreboding gripped him. After a considerable amount of argument, Elsyn and Ben had agreed that they would speak the duke, while Kandar searched for the source of fairy contamination in the house—and the fairy door, if it existed. Ben had given him a drop of blood to open the door and explained the plan of the building.

Turnip, having never been among the fairies, had conflated all of their scents into a single mushroomy nose when she relayed her memories. Kandar, who had spent more time than he would have liked under various fairy hills retrieving stolen goblin treasure and horses and children, could smell at least three distinct traces. One of these had been laid down in the last day on the floor of the corridor. He wondered how the corruption had been worked—if different fairies came through here every night to work their mischief on cheeses and humans, or if a solitary fairy was busy laying enchantments on people and objects that would last for weeks.

He emerged into the service courtyard, blinked at the sunlight, and then continued immediately into the house. A faint and intriguing trace led upward into the mansion proper. That one smelled like a specific charm attached to a person; it was stale and flat, like a spell-bag filled with withered ingredients.

The intense, less-than-a-day-old smell, which he was increasingly sure belonged to an actual fairy and not a bespelled human, took a sharp left onto the cellar stairs and descended. Kandar descended too, excited and increasingly bloodthirsty. The sooner the fairy kingdom was permanently disentangled from Elsyn's, the sooner he could get on with the more enjoyable parts of being prince-consort.

The stairs descended past one level of cellars, then two, then three, where they stopped in a blank floor. The vaults of each were resoundingly empty, but for a thick layer of dust and the smell. Kandar heard water dripping on the third level down and guessed this must be the cistern Ben had mentioned in his description of the house. The smell of fairy magic was everywhere around him, but Kandar couldn't see where in the barren, vaulted space fairies could have hidden a door.

Kandar stopped and itched an ear, thinking about all his previous encounters with the fairy kingdom. There had been a kidnapping attempt when he was still a child. The elven chevalier had placed Kandar in a garden surrounded by four rings of walls, each with four doors and four locks and four guardians who asked four riddles. The goblin king his cousin beheaded the knight, while the witch Ashmallen had incinerated two of the guardians with magical fire. The rest had fled, and the whole structure collapsed into a heap of ashes. The three of them had wended their way back to the mountains just-up-and-to-the-left through an undifferentiated mess of fog and shadow.

That was the trouble; fairies found him, not the other way around. Usually a fairy appeared in a perfectly ordinary place, looking perfectly ordinary, holding something that a child would like to have. Then, once the child's attention transfixed by the perfectly carved model of a horse with articulated joints, the fairy could ease away into a side-tunnel that led Somewhere Else. The child, goblin or human, did not notice the terrain changing around them, so intently did they focus on the toy painted exactly to look like Socks, until they were totally in the fairy world.

Kandar scowled.

The trick was to notice one thing, but not all things; to let go of one's sense of the world around and let the fairy magic change reality as it would.

He didn't like it, and he liked it even less when he returned to the stairs and found that they now continued downward, where they hadn't before. The fairy king and his daughter had done their best to neutralize all possible threats to her power—buying or glamouring those nobles who could be corrupted, methodically destroying one temple after another, cloistering Elsyn, banishing Ben. Of course they had a plan to deal with Ben's mother, who had seen the false Taryn as the monster she was. One his daughter had been killed and the fairy door in the palace closed, Oberon had every reason to open this one wider and send more and weirder magic through.

Footsteps echoed behind him, and Kandar's head jerked up.

"My mother isn't here," Ben said from above him. He held a lantern that cast an orange circle of light.

"We've looked through all the bedrooms and kitchens," Elsyn said. "None of the priests or the servants have seen her leave, and we thought—did she pass by you in the servants' tunnel?"

Kandar shook his head silently.

"Have you found it?" Ben asked, before coming to stand beside him. He looked down into the darkness, nonplussed, before turning to look over his shoulder. "I thought we'd come down three flights."

"You have."

Ben frowned at him. "But there's nothing below the third cellar. The stairs end there."

"That," said Kandar, "is the door into the fairy kingdom."

Elsyn stared down into the dark stairwell. "So this is where fairies have been coming and going all this time," she said quietly.

"I think it very likely, yes," Kandar said.

She took a deep breath, but she felt overwhelmingly sick. "Do you think all the noble houses are riddled with fairy tunnels? We might close the doors out in the fields and hedges, but there's no way the Glascrann or the lesser Deragcaish will allow anyone into their strongholds."

He rubbed a thumb over his tusks thoughtfully. "I don't know," he said finally. "There are laws which fairies have to follow, about human-built walls and ownership and invitations." He crouched and dipped his hand through where the floor ought to be, as though he were testing the temperature of a bath. "I think this is only here because it's technically at the very end of the house, and the humans didn't lay stones to build this cellar, but chiseled it out of rock that was already here."

"Could Algenymmar have gone down there?" Ben asked.

Both of them looked at Kandar. He grimaced. "There's no reason she should," he said. "But I'd lay odds on it. They wouldn't let the tunnel open so easily if there wasn't some reason for us to follow it down."

"So it's a trap," Elsyn said.

"Yes," Kandar said.

The two of them looked at Elsyn for a very long moment. In the dim light, she could see lines of strain of Ben's mouth, and a deep line between Kandar's eyebrows.

She stepped down onto the first of the fairy stairs.

"Elsyn," Ben said, "if you are doing this for me, you need not—"

The thought of any number of fairies passing in and out of the ducal house unseen made Elsyn's heart hammer and her ears ring. It was one thing to imagine an inanimate magic oozing up through a hole in the ground, warping the things and people around it, but the thought of so many active, malicious intelligences of unknown power floating about in her kingdom terrified her. The false Taryn had done so much damage alone in the human world. She could not imagine what the kingdom that had produced her looked like. "Even if I was only doing it for you, you'd have no right to stop me," she snapped. "You are—you are my beloved friend, and she's your *mother*. I'd do anything to have my own mother back, and she wasn't half the woman Algenymmar is." She choked on the last word and pinched the bridge of her nose so she wouldn't cry. "She's been a monster to you, and this time when I find her I'm going to force her to apologize, but I can't leave her."

"I—you—" Ben looked back at Kandar. "Kandar, I cannot ask you—"

"You can. You are also precious to me," he said, and there was an odd note in his voice. "I, too, would like to have my mother back, if I could."

Elsyn took another step down the fairy stairs. Fear of the darkness and what lay within it made her knees shake. "Kandar, what was your mother like?"

He understood the question for what it was—*tell me I am not alone in this*—and so he spoke steadily as they descended, narrating the life of Usdar, daughter of Erlar, terror of gods, speaker to storms, occasional singer to ghosts and chess-player with gryphons. She had arrived in the goblin mountains with the other horse-lords a very long time ago, even by goblin standards, who reckoned time much more slowly than humans did. The few remaining goblins then had been so tired and full of grief that they had retreated to the deepest caves below their castle and turned to stone. The horse-lords, who had come from a land very far away with no goblins at all, had thought them to be statues honoring the ancestors of a people long departed from the peaks. They carried shrines to their foremothers with them and cared for the memory of their dead hosts in the same way: hanging their necks with flowers and offering them mare's milk and mountain irises.

This was, of course, just the sort of magic to wake a goblin whose heart had become granite. Usdar had just poured a libation of wine into the lap of Kandar's father when he opened his eyes and swore at her.

"Or so I have been told," he added.

For the first ten flights of fairy stairs, they appeared just the same as the human-built ones into the cellar—carved from stone, covered in dust, with a deep depression worn into the center by hundreds of years of feet walking up and down them. But as Elsyn grew more involved in Kandar's story of the horse-lords and his mother Usdar, the walls began to shift. First she caught hints of flickering green in the corners of her eyes. These resolved themselves into glowing lichens which spread over the wall in overlapping rosettes. Next came flashing lights: reflections of the light from Ben's lantern glancing off large chunks of crystal embedded in the stone.

When Kandar told them of the silver-winged gryphon from whom his mother had won a miniature mechanical goose, its wings so perfect it could fly around her head and bite her ears, the stairs turned into a true tunnel with a sloping floor. When he described the six-legged, fire-breathing horse she had stolen from the god of summer storms, the stone of the tunnel's wall changed to earth. Roots poked through the ceiling and brushed the tops of their heads.

When Kandar spoke slowly and in careful syllables of how Trosvar, the mother of the king of goblins, had fallen deep into a chasm of ice, and her younger sister Usdar had descended to pull her free, curling green vines grew over the earthen walls, peculiar leaves and flowers unfolding from each one.

Kandar stopped speaking, and Elsyn realized that the light ahead of them had materialized into a carved wooden gate, beyond which a dense mass of vegetation blocked any further sight.

"And what happened then?" Ben asked.

"I don't know," Kandar said. "Neither of them came back."

Ben's heart drummed faster when he saw the gate. Tendrils of ivy wrapped each of the curving pieces of wood, such that it was hard to tell where the barrier started and the plants around it ended. He stepped forward and laid his left hand against it, glancing back at Kandar and Elsyn. Both gave him a little nod, and he pushed the gate open.

The space on the other side was difficult to see, let alone parse into recognizable shapes. Plants, vines, trees, flowers, roots, leaves, stalks were everywhere, making a dense vegetal enclosure. Thousands of shades of green glowed around them as if lit from above by the noonday sun, but he didn't think the sun had anything to do with this. The distressingly peculiar thing was that none of the plants would stay still; they constantly formed themselves into familiar shapes, which then dissolved and reformed again. He watched a vine wrap itself into an ornate, throne-like chair, and then a moment later it was a window looking out over an ocean —the white-crested waves painted by dozens of white and blue flowers clustering together for a minute—and then it was a saddle on a rearing horse.

He noticed that Elsyn looked rather queasy, her lips pressed together tightly and her cheeks unusually pale, and Kandar looked more inscrutable than usual, his ears ticking back and forth furiously.

"If you've any silver or iron, it would be best to get hold of it now," the goblin said suddenly. "They know we're here—that's why it's changing like this."

"So now they spring the trap," Ben said, half-drawing the knife in his belt. He hadn't wanted to bring a sword into his mother's house, especially when he meant to start a fight with her.

Kandar shook his head. "Maybe not. The fairies aren't—even they don't always know why they do what they do. Sometimes they're obliged by some ancient charm to act a certain way, even if they don't remember the charm and it's directly counter to what would suit them in the moment." He gestured at a large cluster of mushrooms which had suddenly sprung up in a gap between two tree trunks. The vines and leaves around them were rapidly turning gold, then brown, then crumbling to dust. "The fairy hills themselves have what you'd call personalities, and they have their own opinions about how things are to be done."

"How will we find her, then?" Elsyn asked, sounding as bewildered as Ben felt.

"It's usually not a matter of *finding*," Kandar said wryly. "More of staying alive until the hill decides to bring you to what you're looking for."

They walked forward into the shifting green. Without discussing it, Elsyn took hold of both of their elbows. The pressure of her hand was welcome; the plants moved so quickly that Ben felt himself getting dizzy. He looked back at her. Her face was tense, her lips pressed together tightly.

Ahead of them, he saw there was a place of stillness, where the seething mass let itself form into proper, slender tree trunks, upright and covered in peeling white bark. A flash of red showed through the silvery leaves shimmering around them.

His stomach twisted into a hard knot as they drew closer. A coat of Deragcaish red had been hung in one of the trees, looking very threadbare at the hems and elbows. His mother had always worn a coat like that when she was doing her morning accounts.

"They're taunting us," Kandar said softly. "Be on your guard."

The trees made a sort of corner, and beyond that another space opened, this one lighter and airier, though no less green. The branches of many trees met overhead to form a vault, and the constant shifting of plants from one shape to another was confined to the deep undergrowth.

Four individuals lay sprawled across the moss-plush ground. Two of them were like enormous insects, wearing waistcoats and knee breeches over iridescent carapaces, delicately-veined wings protruding from their backs. They watched the intruders with faceted red eyes, gleaming like a hundred mirror shards, their languid forms akin to enormous dragonflies. Another fairy had a fox's nose and ears and tail, but human eyes and hands and feet. This one was dressed in enormous dress of green velvet and brocade with stuffed sleeves and wide panniers.

The last one stared at them directly. He was a delicate-looking fellow, his skin, hair, and clothes all of gleaming silver. His eyes were dark, like tarnish, and he had very long, sharp teeth. All four held goblets of gold and long golden forks, which they used to skewer fruit off a platter between them.

"Welcome, darlings!" the silver fairy called. "Welcome to my lord's domain!"

"Who is your lord?" Ben asked, and the fairies all laughed.

"To what do we owe the pleasure of a visit from the Queen, her Prince-consort, and their … *subordinate?*" murmured one of the insects, putting the most offensive drawl possible on the last word.

Ben knew that one ought not give a name freely to the fairies, but he was suddenly out of patience. He felt the same anger he had felt when he realized his mother had let her servants attack Elsyn. How *dare* they be so careless of the harm they had caused? "We seek the Duke of Deragcaish," he said, his voice too loud. The fox-lady flinched. "Where would you suggest we look?"

"Do you want to play a game?" the silver gentleman asked, and suddenly there was a rattling silver cup in his hand.

"Are the dice loaded?" Ben asked. Kandar thumped his shoulder warningly.

The fairies laughed again, their voices jangling together like a bouquet of knives. "Of course!" the silver fairy purred.

"Then I don't want to play," Ben said. Elsyn made a little noise of distress behind him. He found her hand and squeezed it.

"Let's make a deal," said one of the insects. "A game of knucklebones, best of three. If you win, we'll tell you what you want to know. If you lose, you have to ask the truth-tree for answers."

The other fairies laughed raucously. Ben looked over his shoulder at Kandar, who grimaced but nodded slightly.

Knucklebones was an unpleasantly simple dice game, generally used by hucksters and soldiers who wanted to get out of taking watch. Each player called their number, between one and six; four dice were rolled, and the number that came up the greatest number of times won that round. Elaborate rules governed who won if neither number came up, having to do with multiples, subtraction, and the day of the week, but Ben doubted they would be needed.

"Call your number," the silver fairy said languidly.

"Four," he said.

"Six," his opponent said. The fox-fairy dashed the fruit off the golden platter into the moss, where it disappeared. The silver fairy tossed the dice out on the platter: two fours and two sixes.

"A draw," he said, showing all his teeth in a nasty smile. "Call your number."

"One," Ben said.

"Three," the fairy said, tossing the dice again. They rattled slowly around the platter, finally falling to a single three and three fives.

"You might yet win," the fox-fairy said in mock charity.

"Choose wisely," said the insect. "The truth-tree bears strange fruit." The four of them cackled.

Ben thought about grabbing the golden platter and smashing it down on the silver fairy's head, but that seemed like it might backfire. "Four again," he said.

"Five," said the fairy. The dice clicked across the plate: four fives. The fox-fairy and the insects squealed with laughter, the noise twisting into inhuman shapes.

Even though he had known this was an elaborate joke, that he had never had a chance of winning, Ben felt the pit of his stomach drop.

"You win, sir," he said, as coolly as he could muster. "Tell me how I might find the truth-tree."

The two insects buzzed their wings, launching themselves into the air. As they flew they diminished in size, letting their velvet liveries fall to the ground, where they became humps of moss. The fox-fairy dove forward out of her gigantic dress, sliding noiselessly into a complete, fine-pawed fox body. The dress sagged to one side, then burst into a cloud of white seeds like dandelion fluff.

The silver gentleman stood, clicked the heels of silver shoes together, spun around, and abruptly was not there. In his place now grew a gnarled little tree, only as tall as Ben's shoulder. Small red fruits hung from every branch.

"Kandar?" he asked. "Do you know how we're supposed to ask it questions?"

The goblin crouched by the tree and sniffed a fruit. "I haven't the slightest idea."

"O honored truth-tree, do you know where Alg—where the Duke of Deragcaish is, and can you tell us where how we can find her?" Elsyn asked, hands on her hips, frowning at the tree.

"I don't think that—" Ben started to say, at the same moment that three glistening fruits dropped from the tree's branches and rolled toward them.

They looked down at the fruit, then at each other. "Is this a trick?" Elsyn asked. Her thick brows drew down over her eyes, and Ben very much wanted to rub his thumb over her forehead until she took a deep breath and her shoulders dropped.

"It's *always* a trick, but there's no way of knowing until we eat them whether they'll make us fart for a month or fall asleep for a hundred years," Kandar said. "Great good gods, I *hate* fairies, and I hate being under a fairy hill." His tail whipped angrily, and his ears lay flat against his skull. An enormous tenderness warmed Ben's chest, and he bit back a laugh. He didn't think Kandar meant to joke.

"Is it worth it, then?" Ben asked. "If we don't know if the tree will answer the question?"

"It will answer the question, because fairies don't lie," Kandar said immediately. "It's just a question of what *else* it will do to us."

An irrational, mad thought crept into his mind: It will be all right, because we are here together. It was a foolish thought—plenty of lovers died with each other when a ship sank or an army was routed or a house was burned—but it gripped his heart and steadied him. He picked up a fruit.

The fruit, of course, tasted wonderful. The flesh was as soft as a peach, as tart as a gooseberry, and as sweet as an apple. Kandar licked the juice off his lips and shot a nervous look at Elsyn and Ben. Both were still chewing. They didn't yet look unwell. He held out his hands and inspected his claws. They didn't grow into loops or transform into frogs. He jumped up to touch the branches arching above, landing on all fours without losing his balance.

The tree rapidly shrunk back into the moss, while a ring of red- and purple-capped mushrooms grew around where it had been. Kandar growled involuntarily. He loathed all the unnecessary transformation of *this* into *that* and the gratuitous swapping of a *strange thing* for a *slightly different and weirder thing*. Showing off as a personality was something a person was supposed to leave behind in adolescence, not make into the organizing concept for an entire world.

He paced around the clearing, wondering how the fruit was supposed to communicate—

—until suddenly, he knew which direction to go.

"*There*," yelped Elsyn, and he knew what she meant and knew that Ben knew what she meant.

Kandar whirled and dashed across the clearing, toward the sure sense of *there, go there*. He could hear Ben and Elsyn behind him, tearing through the plants that did not move quickly enough out of their way. The fairy hill shifted around them, bringing some things close and pushing others farther away. *There* jumped from one side of the hill to the other, but he ran on, making abrupt switchbacks, hurtling over ponds, scaling small houses, and diving through the bases of clock-towers built of wisteria vines. Once he jumped a family of badgers sitting around a stump set with a full porcelain tea service, and they cursed him roundly.

He had lost Elsyn and Ben, but he could feel and sometimes see both of them chasing the *there* along their own paths through the fairy hill. They were each of them methodical hunters, and the *there* was slowly pinioned between them, trapped until the hill could not move without one of them catching it.

He skidded to a stop at the same time that Elsyn and Ben halted suddenly, certain in the knowledge that they had cornered the *there*. They stood around another tree, this one much more massive than the truth-tree. Set into its base was a round door, painted red, with brass hinges and a brass lock. Kandar jabbed his finger in the keyhole. It did not open.

"What are you *doing?*" a voice said from above. "Running around like rabbits with brain rot!"

"We've—got—to—*find*—" Elsyn gasped, bent double.

A gigantic raven, its head as big as Kandar's, its wingspan as wide as he was tall, hopped down from a high branch. "That door won't open until the sundown fairy makes their rounds on the other side," it said.

"And how long will that be?" Kandar asked. He was starting to feel decidedly odd. Not sick, just … odd.

"I would have no way of knowing, of course," said the raven, "but in four hours, twenty-seven minutes, and thirty-three seconds, you ought to be ready."

"Four *hours?*" repeated Elsyn. "I wish I'd brought a cheese manual to read."

Kandar laughed loudly, surprising himself. The odd feeling was spreading from his head down into his neck and shoulders. Ben laughed as well, and that made Kandar laugh more.

"You won't need it," said the raven. "You've just come from the truth-tree, haven't you?"

Kandar felt too light for his stomach to sink, but he thought he understood why the four fairies had been so amused by causing the three of them to eat the truth-tree's fruit. "We have."

"I expect you're experiencing the most common side effect," the raven said, clacking its beak. "You'll be busy until the door opens."

"Busy with what?" Ben asked. His face was flushed, and he wrinkled his nose at Elsyn. She wrinkled her nose back.

"The tree reveals all kinds of truths, particularly the ones that would be embarrassing to admit to your grandmother later," the bird said. "Watch for the door to open!" It spread its wings and jumped into the air, before flapping away ponderously.

Kandar fell to all fours again, a little shakily. Elsyn knelt down next to him and stroked his back, and Ben crouched and gently felt around his skull. "Are you all right?"

He sprawled slowly on the moss. "I think my head is going to float off without me," he said. This didn't seem too bad. He couldn't imagine being embarrassed about anything he might say to these two people, who he loved—loved!—and also who he wanted to rub his face on, most of the time. All of the time.

He realized, a bit belatedly, that he'd said that last bit out loud.

"Which of us are you talking to?" Elsyn asked, leaning over him.

"Both of you," Kandar said. "Would you take your clothes off?"

"Both of us?" Ben asked.

Kandar nodded. There was some reason why Elsyn wouldn't want to do that, but he couldn't remember what it was. He reached up and touched both of their faces, outlining chins and noses and eyebrows with each hand. "I could smell you more clearly if you did."

Ben had started pulling off his boots. "Is that a good thing?" he asked, laughing again.

"Yes," Kandar said firmly.

Elsyn's mind was strangely blank. Kandar was stretched out in front of her, graceful and lazy as a panther, his eyes half-open. He looked more relaxed than she'd ever seen him. Ben, too, was happy, a smile creasing his face as he lined up his boots and hung his doublet on the branch of a tree. Her shoulders dropped away from her ears, and her jaw felt like she had been clenching it until only very recently. Why had she been so worried? She had her two people, and they were whole and healthy and safe.

"What are the chances of fairies stealing our clothes?' she asked. There was some reason she was generally very anxious about this sort of thing, and she couldn't think what it was. Was it the possibility of clothing theft? It certainly wasn't Ben, who had now stripped off his linen shirt. She had not seen his body in a long time, not since they had both been children, and she looked at him carefully, noting new scars on his torso, tufts of hair growing on his shoulders, and the thick muscles of his arms and chest.

Ben realized she was looking and spread his arms wide, turning slowly so she could see him from all sides.

"You're beautiful," she said, and then, "I love you."

"That's good," he said, laughing, "because I love the both of you also."

She looked down at Kandar where he lay on the moss. "You should also take your clothes off."

He sat up and began unbuttoning his collar and cuffs with great efficiency. He pulled his shirt off and asked, "Do you love me?"

"No," said Elsyn. "I think I will in another week." Those words felt heavy as they left her mouth, and she hoped they did not strike him too sharply.

"I would like it to be now," Kandar said plaintively.

"I know," she said.

"Maybe Ben and I can fuck you and tell you that you are beautiful and wonderful and good until you love me too," he suggested.

That sounded like a nice idea, though she was foggy on its mechanics. "I think I have to check on my cheeses before you would be done," she said. "Perhaps we should get a start now and take it up again later."

Her robe took a bit more effort to remove, and Ben helpfully moved behind her and tugged it up over her head once she had pulled the hem free of her folded legs. He knelt behind her, put his arms around her waist, and pressed his face into her hair. She looked at Kandar gravely. "I am glad it was you who the goblin king sent. I don't think I could want anyone besides the two of you."

Kandar's eyes sparkled, and his lips twitched. "I will likely want many others, but never two so much."

"Mrmph," Ben said against Elsyn's neck.

Kandar leaned forward and pushed his face between her breasts. This was a thing he seemed to like very much, Elsyn thought dimly. He took hold of both of them, one in each hand, playing with the nipples with his thumbs. She drew a deep breath, and Ben took his nose away from her neck long enough to kiss her jaw.

They moved slowly together, careful but not tentative. Elsyn found that she wanted to take care of the two of them so much that her stomach hurt with it. She put her hand over Ben's where it gripped the flesh of her belly and kissed the top of Kandar's head, then took hold of his ears and lifted his face until it was even with hers.

"Show me how to touch you."

"I am happy to serve my queen," Kandar said, his voice so low she felt it more than heard it.

"Do what your queen tells you," Elsyn whispered back. "Show me."

Ben's hand moved under hers, tugging the front of Kandar's trousers open. Elsyn looked down and blinked, startled. She had a vague memory from—when?—of sneaking a look at Ben's private bits, but she didn't recall them being quite so substantial.

Maybe that memory was an old one, because Ben was slowly

rubbing something that felt equally large against her bare back. She reached behind her and touched his hip gently, then let him shape her fingers around Kandar. She looked into the face before her, memorizing the way the small muscles ticked around his mouth and eyes as her hand moved up and down. Goblins did not sweat, but his mouth was open, and he was panting.

Kandar wrapped his hand around hers and began to move it more vigorously. He laid his forehead on her shoulder. At the same time Ben started to move his hips more quickly against her back.

There was now a warm stickiness on her back and on her hand, and she opened her mouth to ask what had happened, but Kandar looked up and pressed his face to her open lips, so instead she gently bit the tip of his nose.

One of Ben's hands traveled over her thigh, pulling her legs a little wider and stroking down through the soft black hair that grew between them. At the same time, the knuckles of Kandar's right hand, his claws curled into his palm, firmly took hold of her sensitive nub and worked it in a steady rocking motion.

One of them—Elsyn, coasting along on an edge of euphoria, wasn't sure whose hand it was—pushed two fingers into her. She sucked in her breath in discomfort. "No, that's—that hurts—" The fingers were withdrawn, and both Kandar and Ben pressed so tightly against her it felt like they might accidentally meld into some sort of three-headed beast. Their hands were rubbing—faster—and then—

Elsyn let out a little cry, and her body shivered with release. She was hot and damp and realized she had been holding her breath for the last several minutes as she gasped for air.

Very slowly, the three of them tipped over onto the moss like a felled tree.

The small red door in the tree led directly into Oberon's throne room. Ben did not need Kandar's panicked whisper in his ear to know this; he pieced it together from the chained manticore and sphinx on either ends of the dais, the hundreds of fairies in elaborate court dress, and above all the great bejeweled crown atop the head of the fairy on the throne.

Oberon was another one of the insect-like fairies, though his portly form was more beetle than a dragonfly. He had very large mandibles, which clicked while he talked. He talked constantly.

They stepped out into the throne room proper, and Ben noticed that there were alcoves like the one they had just emerged from perforating the room at regular intervals on all sides. Fairies and other creatures passed into and out of the room continuously. A fairy shaped like a pig dragged a brace of screaming unicorns haltered with golden chains past them, their opalescent hooves kicking the air in fury.

Elsyn startled backwards and bumped into him. Ben put a hand to her back to steady her, then quickly dropped it when she found her feet. They did not meet each other's eyes. His palm itched where he had touched her. No, his whole body itched. He wanted in equal measures to howl into the room that his queen loved him, did they all know that, would they all shut up and listen because *his queen loved him*, and to crawl into a hole and never come out. He was not married to Elsyn. Kandar was married to Elsyn. He had let go of an irrevocable truth, and there was no way they could choose not to know how he stood with each of them. They would either die down here or return to the human kingdom above, and if it ended up being the latter he had no idea what possible place there was for him.

This, then, was the trick the truth-tree had played on them.

Kandar caught his eye and raised his eyebrows. Ben raised his eyebrows back, and Kandar looked toward the throne and rolled his eyes elaborately. A little laugh bubbled up in Ben's tight chest.

They hadn't survived yet, he told himself. They hadn't even discovered whether his mother was really here, or if this was all an elaborate goose-chase. He had to focus on that first.

It was then that Oberon looked out through the crowd and shouted, in an earth-shattering voice, "My good Queen Elsyn! My dear Prince Kandar! You honor my court with your presence."

The room did not grow quiet—there were too many screeching, snarling creatures for that—but the begowned and besuited courtesans parted as smoothly as hay cut by a scythe, opening a path up to the dais.

Elsyn glanced to her left and her right, then squared her shoulders and walked imperiously toward the throne. Ben closed his eyes for a moment before he followed, three steps behind her and two behind Kandar. Gods, they were impressive.

"Of course," Oberon went on, in his ear-splitting scream, "I have hosted your family before. Your sister made her home with me for *eleven years*." He shrieked, and it took Ben a moment to realize the king was laughing.

"I am aware, O King Under the Hill," said Elsyn. She did not so much as flinch. "Where is my subject Algenymmar, who you have stolen from me?"

Oberon shrieked with laughter again. He kicked something with his foot out to the edge of the dais, where it flopped limply. Ben squinted, unable to see what the object was. They walked closer. The throne room was very long, and he guessed fairy magic had stretched it out to be even more impressive.

The object was a human hand, attached to a human wrist, attached to a human body that lay half-crumpled under Oberon's throne. The signet ring had been torn off, leaving the middle finger swollen and bruised, but as soon as Ben understood that it was a hand, he knew whose hand it was.

"Let us make a deal," Oberon said, his voice wheedling. "You may have her as she is and go free, or you may leave her with me for a hundred years." He clicked his mandibles gleefully. "Of course, I don't imagine you can get her back through the wood and up all those stairs before all her blood leaks out. She was not *at all* respectful to my knights when I sent them to fetch her."

"And if she stays?" Elsyn said levelly. She walked steadily forward, and Ben followed, focusing on the back of her head and breathing through his nose.

"Then all of my finest doctors will attend her immediately," Oberon murmured, if a murmur could happen at a pitch and volume that threatened to make Ben's ears bleed. "I will so appreciate improving my acquaintance with a woman who frustrated my daughter's efforts for so very long." He reached down to touch the body beneath his throne with a finger like a beetle's claw. "She will *so* appreciate hearing about my little tricks. I don't think she suspects I sent the envoy who so captivated her son, nor took him away neither. And to think, she banished her own child over it!"

Oberon looked directly into Ben's eyes with his shimmering ones, and Ben knew that the king knew he was here and who he was.

"I can hardly credit that they took that bag of leaves and turnip for a *body*," he went on crooning. "Why, when darling Aubrey was here safe all the time!" He waved his beetley little hand, and a fairy knight appeared at his side. It took Ben a long moment to recognize the fairy's face, for the eyes had gone strange and the ears long and pointed.

"Perhaps she will not remember at all," Elsyn said coldly. "It has been seven years."

"I think she will," Oberon scream-laughed. "I think she will. There have been fairies in that house every day since she lost her son, singing her shame in her sleep, embroidering her dreams with his crimes. I think she will have cause to regret how very rude she was to my daughter." He clicked his mandibles, and the fairy knight who had once been a charming human envoy bowed and vanished into another alcove.

The three of them had reached the edge of the dais. Ben stared down at the body. It didn't look like his mother, because he had never seen his mother sprawled on her side, her limbs at awful angles, her face bloodless, her black hair a tangled, dusty mess. He wondered if Algenymmar was already dead.

"Your daughter, who spent eleven years as usurper in my sister's place," Elsyn said.

"Hardly, hardly," Oberon said, with a chuckle like bones rattling. "My daughter made it *her own*."

"Your daughter is dead, and I am queen," she returned, as steadily as if she were asking another priest to pass her a piece of cheesecloth. "We will take Algenymmar."

She and Kandar both stepped out of Ben's way as she said the duke's name. He took the pouch from his belt and threw a cup of salt into the face of Oberon, King of the Fairies.

Several things happened all at once.

The courtesans' voices rose to a deafening racket, and Kandar flattened his ears in an attempt to keep out some of it. The courtesans had apparently not decided yet whether they would slaughter the intruders or not; many of them had drawn out their blades, and he saw a few creeping closer to the dais, their eyes on the crown now sliding off the king's head. Kandar drew his knife, and wished very much for his sword.

Oberon's body deflated like a horrible slug, black liquid oozing out of dozens of tiny holes in his carapace where the salt had touched him. Screaming emanated from his person, but not from his mouth; instead it seemed to be coming from somewhere around his abdomen. Then, just as quickly, he began to shrink, until he was the size of a pig, then a dog, then a cat, then a very large, horrible bug. Kandar leaped, trying to smash the thing under his foot, but it scuttled away into the gap beneath the throne. He flung the throne to one side, but the insect-king had vanished into a crack in the stone of the dais.

Elsyn hauled herself up next to Ben and gathered up Algenymmar's limp upper body in her arms. She had produced a small package from somewhere—where had she been keeping that?—opened it, and took out something white, which she held to the duke's lips.

A terrific, ear-splitting whinny cut through the stuffy air under the fairy hill, followed by a trumpeting *moo*. Socks burst through one of the alcoves, fairies scrambling to get out of the way of his iron-shod hooves. He had reluctantly agreed to the shoes the day before the wedding. Just behind him stamped Turnip, who tossed her head and thundered.

Hello hello hello! Hello, we have come to rescue you! Turnip has led me here! I am very smart and brave and I will kick many fairies in the teeth!

"*Socks,*" Kandar gasped. He had just seen something truly awful. The golden ring with which the manticore's chain was fixed to the wall had been snapped in half and now swung empty. A cacophony of screaming accompanied its progress through the room. Fairies were not particularly good eating, and the moment the monster's eyes fixed on Socks it slavered with greed. The manticore sprung at the horse, chattering rows and rows of teeth. It clamped onto his hindquarters, tearing his hide with its lion's paws. Socks screamed and reared, trying fling off the attacking beast. The manticore's scorpion tail flashed over its shoulder, but Kandar jumped, slicing with his knife, and the poisonous tip clattered to the ground.

Socks' neigh had seemed to split the court in half, but it was nothing compared to the noise that echoed under the hill now. Three horses with three riders sprang through the largest alcove. Kandar could have wept when he saw the first one, a great black mare with six legs and smoke curling from her nose. She gathered her legs beneath her and jumped to the center of the room, where the great horse seized the manticore in her teeth and dashed it against the floor.

It shuddered and fell still.

True silence descended for a single moment, and then the fairies fled the throne room.

The goblin king grinned down at Kandar, and Kandar, in spite of himself, grinned back up at his cousin.

Algenymmar was badly hurt, but as Elsyn had suspected, not quite so near death as the king had boasted.

She didn't know what had possessed her to wrap a piece of the moon-cheese and tie it up in her shift, but when she pushed a bit of it into the duke's mouth, the other woman's skin suddenly became more lifelike than waxy, and her bones rearranged themselves into the proper shape. Elsyn put another piece of cheese on the duke's tongue, and Algenymmar gasped and started to breathe regularly. She had a nasty black eye and, based on how she shuddered when Elsyn moved her, at least one broken rib.

"You—she—" Ben was standing over her. He crouched to look at his mother's face.

"She's not dead," Elsyn said quickly. "It's going to be a mess to move her, though, she's got some things broken—"

"Let us help," someone said from the edge of the dais.

Elsyn's body filled with ice and then fire and then ice again before her thinking mind had even recognized the voice. She thought she might be sick, but then she'd have to clean vomit off of Algenymmar. Maybe she could crawl to the edge of the dais and retch there.

No.

She was queen.

Ben and Kandar were with her, and Turnip was not far away.

She had just faced the King of the Fairies and revived the duke of Deragcaish from a sleep like death.

She looked up.

It was, in some way, like the first moment she had seen Ben again, standing stiffly in the doorway of the cheese-making room. Taryn could be no one else, but she looked nothing like any of Elsyn's memories of her—neither the child who had really been her sister, nor the sickly copy that Oberon's daughter had pretended to be. This Taryn wore a goblin coat of brilliant blue belted over loose trousers. Her face was brown and round, not pale and hollowed, like the creature who had taken such pleasure in hurting Elsyn.

The real Taryn was still not as tall as Elsyn, but she looked— sturdy. Healthy.

Taryn smiled at her, and the expression was oddly tentative. Elsyn wondered what her own face was doing, but surely she was staring wild-eyed, like she had seen a ghost.

She *had* seen a ghost.

"Ben," Taryn said, a little stiffly. "It has been a long time. I am happy to see that you are well."

He nodded to her, seemingly unable to speak.

"Ashmallen can help with the duke," Taryn said quietly. Elsyn realized there was a short, ruddy-faced person dressed in a shabby leather jerkin and trews standing behind Taryn. They had been at the Elsyn's coronation, half-invisible in the shadows. Ildar had said Ashmallen was a powerful witch, and a very old friend of the goblin king.

They nodded to Elsyn and held up a leather pack. "Got all my supplies here. I'll do what I can for her, and then we'll make up a stretcher." They hoisted themself up and gently extracted Algenymmar from her grasp, laying the duke down flat on her back and brushing her hair away from her face. The witch drew out several packets, murmuring steadily. An odd smell filled the air.

"How did you—" Elsyn shook her head, suddenly exhausted. "How did you get here? How did you know to come?"

"Turnip the cow," Taryn said. "She guessed where you'd gone, so she went to tell Kandar's horse, Kandar's horse told Ildar, and Ildar sent about a hundred palace cats to fetch us." She frowned. "Socks wasn't supposed to come himself—he promised Ildar he wouldn't—"

Elsyn wondered how fetching someone from hundreds of miles away in mountains on a slightly different plain of existence worked. Ashmallen hummed and winked at her.

"Socks isn't a well-behaved horse," she said. "A very good horse, but not well-behaved." She saw Turnip leaning against Socks, licking his injuries, some of which were already disappearing. She wondered again if cows could be magic-users.

"He is the *best* horse," said a gravelly voice by her ear, and Elsyn looked up into Kandar's face.

"Quince is a good gelding," said Ben, his voice thick. He cleared his throat. "I am—I am glad he did not come to rescue me, though. He is old, and I don't think he could fight off a manticore."

"Yes," Kandar said. He looked at Elsyn. "A week, did you say?"

She swallowed hard. "Maybe five days," she said shakily.

He nodded. "Very well." He looked at Ben. "And you are bound by love, and by obligation, and by blood; but if you wish to be married by a goblin shaman in the mountains, tell me, and we will all three ride up together and seek one out."

Elsyn reached unseeing for their hands, taking one in each of hers. She pressed Kandar's palm to her lips, then kissed Ben's, then pressed both against her heart.

The High Priest was sitting on the top cellar step, a lantern on the stone beside them. It cast ghastly shadows over their pale face, but Elsyn suspected that the purplish cast to their skin was from exhaustion.

"You've got her," they said, starting to their feet, as Kandar and Ben emerged from the darkness, carrying Algenymmar in a cloak between the two of them. "Oh, thank the God in Their Bodies."

The terrible mix of grief and joy in their voice made Elsyn go still for a long moment, her foot on the next stair, her eyes searching the High Priest's face.

"Is she—is she," the High Priest said, apparently unable to go on, "Is she—is she?"

The anger Elsyn felt toward the High Priest did not go away, but for a moment it was clouded with understanding. "She is not dead. She will probably be all right. She needs to sleep for a long while."

Kandar clucked behind her, and she hastened up the stairs. "Come on."

The High Priest stared over her shoulder. "Why is there—why is there a horse?"

"Socks is a noble friend," Elsyn said firmly. "And you ought to know Turnip. Come along, please."

The High Priest followed them all the way to the palace, asking panicky questions. Ben could not bring himself to answer, but Kandar and Elsyn kept up a steady stream of brusque responses. "No." "Maybe." "Too many to count." "In a week." Socks went ahead of them, prancing and spinning in circles to clear the street, and Turnip came behind, pointedly nosing onlookers out of the way.

Ildar and Jolar met them at the priest-door. "You are alive," the wizard said, relief plain in his gray face. His eyes slid over the person they carried.

"My mother," Ben said. "Duke Algenymmar. Oberon captured her to draw us down into his kingdom."

"There is another fairy door in the cellars of the duke's house which must be closed," Kandar added. "Ashmallen is working on the other side." Ildar nodded, bowed to Elsyn, and strode through the gate back into the city.

Jolar let out a long, low whistle. "That explains a great deal."

"So it does," Kandar said.

"We need to take my mother someplace safe to recover," Ben said.

"About two hours ago, Petra led fifty priests through here, carrying boxes of cheese," Jolar said. "They've decided to use the palace temple again. I imagine they will be more than happy to look after her."

"I'll look after her," the High Priest interjected, sounding a little desperate.

"You can stay with her," said Elsyn.

Petra was indeed in the main hall of the temple, shouting instructions and wielding a broom like a shepherd's crook to herd the priests this way and that. Her eyes widened as she took in the three of them, and the unconscious duke, and the High Priest.

"The God in Their Bodies," she said. "We'll take her. No—I don't need to know right now. You can explain later. Go and rest."

"Thank you, my friend," Elsyn said, dipping her head deeply.

Ben could not name the emotion that twisted his stomach as he carefully set down his end of the cloak, letting his mother rest on the floor. Six priests immediately put down their boxes and cleaning tools and gathered around her, arguing about medicinal herbs and charms. One of them produced a blanket from nowhere and wrapped it around Algenymmar's body.

"Let's go," Elsyn said softly in his ear.

Napping in the temple with dozens of priests vigorously cleaning it was impossible, and Elsyn did not want to go back into the palace until every room could be checked for magic or purified by priests.

"He's not gone," she said to Kandar. "You know he's not gone. I don't know how long he'll take to regroup, but he'll try again soon."

He thought of the many-legged bug scuttling under the fairy

throne and grimaced. "Ben might have weakened him."

"Maybe," Elsyn said.

"Maybe," Ben echoed.

They found a spot in the tall grass on the opposite side of the temple from the priest-door, between two large rocks that made it inconvenient for the holy herd to leave any dung there, then laid down to sleep.

Elsyn awoke to Kandar nuzzling her neck. It took a moment for her to understand where she was and with whom: on a hill in the pasture, hidden by high grass, the late afternoon light casting long shadows. Her head was pillowed on Ben's outflung arm, and his other hand rested on her breast. Kandar's face was over hers, and she could feel his knees gently squeezing the sides of her torso.

She slid her hand over Ben's on her breast and squeezed it, then turned her head to the side and met his eyes.

Kandar rubbed his tusks along the underside of her throat.

Recent memories cluttered Elsyn's head. Kandar putting his face between her legs in the royal bed. Ben spreading his arms wide for her to admire his body. Kandar holding her breasts. Ben pressed tight against her back, moving steadily.

And then, below those, a steady, ugly drumbeat: the false Taryn's voice. The laughter of her ladies. The words of Elsyn's own mother, which had gone in deep and lodged next to the bone.

She closed her eyes and took a deep breath.

"What was said after we ate the truth-tree's fruits," she started, then faltered.

"True," Ben said suddenly, fiercely, and put his mouth on her neck also.

"True," Kandar said. "And you knew that before you asked."

"Probably," Elsyn said. She remembered another thing that had happened under the fairy hill and swallowed hard. "I think it's going to take me a while to—fully—I'm not sure I can—"

Kandar had a hand under her robe, unlacing her kirtle. "Hm?"

"The last god-rite is consummation," she said. Ben was stroking her stomach in long, slow circles. "And I'm not sure I can—do that. At least, not right now." If two fingers had hurt, she thought, she'd probably pass out during actual penetration.

Ben took his face away from her shoulder for long enough to ask, "How picky is the god-magic?"

"What do you mean?" Kandar successfully loosened the kirtle and pulled it out from underneath her robe.

"Do you know which part triggers the god's blessing?"

Kandar was now cutting the side-seam on her robe with a small knife. Elsyn considered telling him to stop, but a glance down told her that this garment should probably go in the rag-bin anyway.

"It must be when a child is conceived," she said very quietly. She reached up and stroked Ben's hair back from his ear.

"Surely not," Ben said. The arm her head rested on curled tight around her shoulders. "Everyone knows grandfather had no issue until he was fifty and married twenty years, and he was as gods-blessed a king as they come."

Kandar pushed the fabric of the robe aside with a sound of triumph and immediately pressed his face to her breasts.

"There has to be a child at some point," Elsyn pointed out.

"We could work up to it," Ben said.

"There are," he said, his voice muffled, "many things for us to try to gain the god's blessing before then."

"Did it work?" Elsyn asked, sounding dazed.

"Mrmph," said Kandar.

Ben looked up into the darkening blue of the sky and saw that all around them, strange plants with narrow, silvery leaves had twined through the grass, unfurling frothy clouds of tiny white flowers. Other flowers he recognized but knew did not bloom in midsummer or at night had opened between the lacy rafts—red poppies, blue chicory, a vast array of yellow sunflowers.

EPILOGUE

The sea-goblins arrived in the capital city five months later, leading goat-carts filled with dried fish, amphoras of goat cheese, and ropes of seaweed. Telfar walked at their head, carrying a long silver spear and wearing white cowrie shells braided into her crest.

The sea-goblins demanded to see Ben, and then they demanded to be presented to the queen. Their head goat was a giant black buck with arcing horns like hammerswings. The buck, Fishcake, touched noses gravely with Turnip and Bean.

Algenymmar had apologized to Ben, or at least they had spent a long afternoon closeted together, both emerging white-faced and drawn but civil. Ashmallen and Ildar had closed the fairy tunnel in the cellars of the ducal house, but Algenymmar had not returned there, instead retiring to one of the temples just outside the city. The High Priest had not apologized to Elsyn, but they had bowed deeply to her and surrendered their horns of office. They, too, had retired to a temple just outside the city.

Petra acted as interim High Priest, until votes could be collected from all the priests who had been in hiding to confirm her position as permanent. More priests trickled back into the city every day, on foot, in carts, riding mules. The fairy weirdness was not gone, but it had become less pointedly malicious. The last three contaminated cheeses Hinat had found sang drinking ballads continuously, but one of them was always in a different key than the other two.

Two of the nobles who had been given control of royal estates by the false Taryn had abruptly delivered all of their keys, accounts, and tenant leases into Elsyn's hands the week after Algenymmar was rescued from under the fairy hill. She suspected Jolar of making this happen through some combination of threats and blackmail, but she declined to ask about the details.

The servants were less interested than Elsyn had expected them to be in where Ben actually slept each night.

Kandar had helped her send a message by cat into the mountains-just-to-the-left. The cat, an elegant creature with long cream fur and green eyes, returned the next night with a response. When the three of them traveled to the mountains-just-to-the-left to be blessed and bound by a goblin shaman, Taryn would walk together with her sister, and they would talk.

Many things could never be fixed, but maybe some could.

Acknowledgments

(from Juniper)

To the sea, I give all due honor and appropriately-timed sacrifices of dairy products.

No thanks to Potato the Goat, who ate the first three copies of this manuscript.

Acknowledgments

(from Sharon)

As always, I am grateful to M.E.D., who read this book at an early stage and assured me that it was not hideous garbage (I paraphrase).

I very much appreciate the assistance of Rose Lerner in jump-starting this novella, after the stresses of the pandemic turned my brain into pudding.

Many thanks to Rose Fox, who provided an invaluable critique for this manuscript and encouraged me to let my characters talk to one another.

While social media can be a source of anxiety and stress, I am also unspeakably thankful that Twitter and other platforms have allowed me to talk with the people who have enjoyed my writing. The last few years have been strange and often isolating, but it's easier to keep making stuff when I know there are still lots of cool people out there who like cheese as much as I do.

About the author

Juniper Butterworth is an elderly goblin who lives by the sea and eats cheese, bearing only a passing resemblance to Sharon J. Gochenour, a writer and illustrator living in Massachusetts. Between the two of them, they've visited a few places and consumed a few dairy products.

Links to more writing, artwork, blogging, and news can be found on sharonjgochenour.com.

A preview of the next book of the Goblins and Cheese sequence

The Dragon Under the Hill

The woman blocking the path of Ildar's horse was small and round and brown.

"There's a dragon stuck in the hedge," she said.

Jackdaw extended his neck to sniff delicately at her tattered robe, and she pushed him firmly to the side. The horse didn't offer to bite, which was a surprise.

Ildar heaved a sigh of annoyance and turned his gelding so he could get a better look at her. He wished he didn't recognize the garb of the priests of the Two-Bodied God; he probably ought to show her a greater level of courtesy than picking her up by the collar and dropping her on the side of the road. "Holy one, I have pressing business on the goblin road."

"Which is why you're going to come help me get it out of the hedge," she said, folding her arms. "It came down the road, and it wouldn't have if anyone on *your* end had been watching."

Ildar bit back an irritated defense. The goblins had been lax in guarding the mountain road, and things—all sorts of things—had been getting through. The problem had grown steadily worse over the last

187

eleven years, when an impostor fairy queen had sat on the human throne. She had had no interest in giving the border temples the money or the people to guard their flocks from red caps and nucklavees. But the influx had spiraled out of control four months prior, after the real heir to the throne, Elsyn, had been crowned, and the fairy king had vanished. Now there were incursions of strange beasts in the towns closest to the goblin road every week, and Ildar didn't like to think what was hiding in the forests that bordered it. One of his saddlebags was full of copies of maps with different sorts of fairy incursions marked on them in various colors. He hoped the goblin king could make sense of what exactly was happening.

There was one point he could argue. "It isn't a dragon." Dragon territory started on the other side of the goblin kingdom in the mountains-just-to-the-left. Those heights stretched far, far away, getting progressively more out of register with this plane of reality until they barely bore a resemblance to the human world at all. There were no doors a dragon could pass through directly into this realm, and no way one could fly over the goblin stronghold without being noticed.

"It is," the woman said.

"It isn't," Ildar snapped.

"It *is*," she insisted.

"It *isn't*, and if you don't stop arguing with me I'll turn you into a toad," he said. He wasn't the kind of wizard who could do that, but she didn't know he was lying.

She did know. "You won't, and as it is a dragon, I need a magic user to help me get it out of the hedge. Come at once, or I'll tell your horse to throw you."

Ildar cast a wary eye down at Jackdaw. He knew that most of the priests of the Two-Bodied God could speak with cows and other dairy beasts, but the talent generally didn't extend to horses. Jackdaw, however, might throw him just for the fun of it.

He gave in abruptly and with poor grace, swinging himself down from Jackdaw's back. The gelding startled and shied away from him; Ildar thumped his neck impatiently. His throat tightened. Snow, his old mare, had been as warproof an animal as a mortal body could hold, unbothered by magic being performed on her back, missiles going over her head, or toddlers clutching at her mane.

Grieving, Ildar told himself, as he done many hundreds of times before, will take up your whole life if you let it.

"Show me your dragon," he told the small woman.

All things considered, Bo was not overly impressed by the goblin king's wizard. The rumors which had come up from the capital city were odd enough that she had assumed that they had gotten garbled at some point in transmission, but now that he was here there was no mistaking him for anyone other than the fabled figure: a rail-thin man, toweringly tall, with gray skin, hair, and eyes, dressed in a long gray coat, the smell of strange magic rolling off him like . . . well, he smelled like a goat, if she were perfectly honest. Perhaps a goat who dined on rare and strange flowers in the most pristine of mountain meadows, but a goat nonetheless.

He also had the manners of a goat.

"Where's the hedge?" he demanded, stepping too close.

"Don't loom," Bo barked.

To her surprise, he blinked and stepped back. "I thought you'd turn out to be a bit taller, once we were on the same level."

Bo, who had stopped growing upward at age nine, scowled. "No. The hedge is this way. Don't mind the temple goats, they're rude." She turned on her heel and trotted back toward the village square.

The last sentence was aimed at Silly and Hortense, who had both followed her out of the temple and were now busily eating blackberry canes in the roadside ditch. They bleated lustily and threw themselves up the bank after her. The wizard clucked to his horse and then slow hoofsteps thudded against the dry road.

The dragon had gotten stuck at the bottom of the temple field. Calling the barrier around the field a hedge was a bit of an understatement. The dense, impenetrable line of intertwined trees, bushes, and creepers ringing the pasture was twenty feet tall and twenty feet thick. Some of the trees holding it up were a thousand years old, and priests had started adding other woody plants to solidify the growth only a few hundred years after that. A person or a goat could go into the hedge, but where they came out would almost certainly not be in the wheat field on the other side.

The only way into the field was through the temple. Bo led the wizard, the horse, and the goats up the small colonnaded porch and through the sanctuary. It was a very, very old temple, a long stone barn with two wall niches for statues of the Two-Bodied God in the center. Its simplicity was further emphasized by its state of extreme disrepair. She had been patching the cracks in the masonry with lime dust and water since the old priest had disappeared five years ago. She wasn't very good at it, and the walls looked rather like a pack of muddy dogs had shaken their coats out in the center of the room.

Bo glared over her shoulder at the wizard, in case he was thinking of making a rude comment, but he only stared at one of the God's statues, a troubled expression on his face. Hortense and Silly, suddenly annoyed with each other, reared up on their hind legs and cracked their skulls together. The wizard's horse, a shining bay, let out a little scream and threw up his head.

"Oh, don't fuss," she said, at the same moment the wizard said, "Beast."

The horse did not look remorseful. His ears flicked back and he lifted a hoof, his leg quivering as though he couldn't decide which one of them he wanted to kick more.

"Leave him with the ponies," Bo said. "I don't want him to scare the dragon."

The ponies were short and fat and very fierce, and they eyed the equine intruder in their corner of the field with gimlet eyes.

"Down here," she said, picking her way past the two retired milchcows and evading Fol-de-rol and her triplet kids. "Watch that you don't step in the pig wallow." The two small black pigs lifted their snouts from the mud and horked loudly at her.

"Are you sure it's not just another goat that's gotten wedged in there?" the wizard asked skeptically.

Then he stopped speaking, for he had just come nose-to-nose with the dragon.